Mr. MERLIN

Episode 2

Mr. MERLIN
Episode 2

an original novel by William Rotsler
based on a characters created by
Larry Tucker and Larry Rosen
in association with Columbia Pictures
Television

Wanderer Books
Published by Simon & Schuster, New York

for
ALEXIS GILLILAND,
a magician of a different sort

Chapter One

San Francisco can be a magical city, even to those who don't believe in magic. There is a spectacular, or at the very least, interesting view from almost any place. It's called "Everyone's Favorite City," even by those not employed by the Chamber of Commerce.

The great bay—discovered by Sir Francis Drake—is the center of everything visual in San Francisco. Gray Alcatraz, unused and lonely, sits in the midst of dangerous currents, visited only by boatloads of tourists who roam the grim halls and try out the darkness of an isolation cell. Wooded islands are to the north, with the worn brown hillsides breaking through, and almost no buildings.

Bleak, businesslike Oakland can be seen through the girders of the Oakland–Bay Bridge, and sturdy little Yerba Buena Island supports the center of the miles-long structure. Beneath the bridge, on the San Francisco side, young Zachary Rogers walked with his sometimes, would-be, maybe girlfriend, Julie Potter.

"I never get tired of this city," Zac sighed, looking up at the mathematical maze of silvery girders that arched overhead. "There's always something new to see."

Julie looked around and hugged herself. "This isn't exactly the ritziest part of town," she muttered. It was the dock area, which curved around that part of the peninsula, with the touristy Fisherman's Wharf at the north end and a navy base at the other. It was dark and a little cold. "Or the most romantic," she sighed.

But Zac wasn't listening. "This is the most romantic city in America," the sixteen-year-old youth exclaimed. "The Gold Rush, the sea trade to China, Hawaii, the South Pacific. During World War Two, men left here, never to return."

Julie took another look around at the deserted docks. Dark, empty freight cars stood on tracks across the road from the hangar-like dock buildings. There were strings of lights on the bridge but not very many here, at the base of the hill. "Never to return," she muttered, looking at Zac. He was cute, she thought, but boys *did* have the oddest ideas, sometimes, about what a "date" was or wasn't.

"Not to mention all the TV shows," Zac said. He pointed his finger like a gun and fired off a few rounds at hidden enemies. "Pow! Blam! Ka-*pow!*" He grinned at Julie. *"The Streets of San Francisco,"* he said. *"Dirty Harry, Magnum Force, Bullitt!"* He varoomed a bit as they strolled. "You gotta see all the parts of this city, Julie! Not just downtown or the wharf or Union Street. Next time we'll go out to the end of Golden Gate Park. There are some old windmills out there, big ones. And where Cliff House used to be . . ."

Julie sighed. Her idea of a romantic location was some secluded restaurant with ferns and wood and beautiful people looking chic and important. San Francisco was full of delightful little restaurants and not one of them was in this part of town.

"Zac, let's go back. It's getting late."

"Late? Gee, Julie, it's not even nine."

"Zac . . ."

"Oh, okay. Look, we parked Mister Merlin's car up there on that side of the bridge and we can go up this street and cross back under by the anchorage."

Julie looked up. The hill was mostly dark, commercial buildings at first, then apartment houses higher up. "Anchorage?"

"Yeah, where the cables from the bridge come in." Eager to show off his knowledge, Zac continued as they started climbing the hill. "It's a suspension bridge, just like the Golden Gate Bridge. Well, this half of it is." He pointed eastward, to Yerba Buena Island, where the last part of the bridge, in shallower water, was a girder bridge.

"The cables hold everything together. But they must be anchored. There's a small mountain of concrete out on the island and another just up here. Otherwise . . ." He made a wide gesture. "The whole thing goes plop into the bay!"

"Oh," Julie said, looking up at the curving cables high overhead. "I didn't know that." Boys were always trying to impress you with things like that, she thought. She had found it was best to pretend ignorance and let them instruct her. And in this case, she really hadn't thought about it.

They continued the steep climb until they came to a more or less level street. Julie could see the cables angling down from the bridge, which was now supported by a conventional girder structure and great concrete pillars the size of small office buildings. No cars passed them on the street and they walked along on the narrow sidewalk.

"See, that's where they go in," Zac said. The structure was more or less a typical 1930s municipal design, high and blank, with curved corners, stained grimly gray and anonymous as a paper bag in the gutter.

"Yes, Zac," Julie said with some weariness. She had hoped to go see the new romantic movie starring Harrison Ford, but Zac had come up with an idea for "something different."

Zac stopped and put out his arm to stop Julie. "Hey," he said softly, peering into the dimness at the base of the wide anchorage. Another streetlight gleamed on shards of broken glass on the street. There was movement in the shadows, a spot of light moving in the recessed doorway to the building. "Are those . . . is that someone trying to . . ."

"Zac," Julie said warningly, "let's just go back along the street and—"

"Julie!" Zac said, moving close to her, whispering in a sharp, conspiratorial voice. "I think those are burglars, trying to break into the anchorage!"

"Don't be silly, Zac. What's in there to steal?"

That stopped Zac for a moment. "I don't know, but ... but look, they are going inside." They heard the dull clang of metal and saw a few glimmers of light. "I better go call the police," Zac said and started to run back up the street.

"Zac!" Julie called out.

"Hey, whuzzat?" The voice came from the shadows near the cable anchorage. "Hey, look!" Julie turned to see two black-clad figures running toward her, crunching glass under foot.

She screamed and started running awkwardly up the street. Darn these high heels! she snapped at herself. Why am I so vain?

"Julie!" It was Zac, up the street, silhouetted against a street light. "Run, Julie!" He began to move toward her.

"I'm ... trying ..."

"Grab her!" A hand seized her arm and

she was roughly pulled off her feet, spinning around to crash against a large muscular man with a face like a fist. She screamed, her eyes getting big. He clapped a hand over her mouth.

She tried to scream again, and to struggle, but he held her tightly against him, swearing. "Git the other one!" he snarled.

The second man pounded up the street toward Zac, who was cautiously heading toward the struggling girl, until he saw the dull gleam of something in the pursuing thug's hand.

A gun!

"Yipes!" Zac said and turned to run and dodge. There were a few parked cars here, and two trucks. He ran around the front of one truck, but instead of running on up the hill he dodged back, crouching down next to the double rear wheels. His heart was pounding loudly enough to be heard in Berkeley, he thought.

He saw the feet of the thug run past in the street, then he heard the man stop. He heard Julie's muffled struggles and felt miserably helpless.

What to do? What to do?

He thought of the few magic spells he

knew, but none of them seemed right. Oh, Merlin, where are you when I need you?

The thug's footsteps were quiet now as he prowled between the cars up ahead. Zac heard the man holding Julie call out in a hoarse whisper, "He get away?"

"Naw, he's here somewheres," the pursuer said in a normal voice. "Aincha, kid? You're here, *somewheres*. Well, you jist lissen to me, smart guy. We gotcha girl, see? You go for the cops and you ain't got no more girl-friend, hear?"

The thug waited for a few moments, moving quietly around. Zac caught a glimpse of him, a great dark weapon gripped in his hand. The youth ducked back, frowning. Why was the gun so huge?

Zac peeked around again, warily. And gulped. The gun was huge because it had a silencer. A tube almost as long as the weapon itself, attached to the end of an automatic. He could be shot and not even wake up a light sleeper.

He pulled back, trying to make himself part of the truck wheels. Now what? he thought. Oh, if I were only Merlin!

Merlin. Max Merlin. Really Merlin Silvester. Myrddin Wyllt. From the court of King

Arthur. *That* Merlin, as Zac had once put it. *The* Merlin.

The magician.

Alive, today, sixteen hundred years after his birth in Wales. "My father was an incubus and my mother a Welsh princess," Merlin had told him on that fateful day not long ago. Merlin then had also told him the Dreadful Secret.

Merlin needed an apprentice ... and Zachary Rogers was it.

All because Zac had pulled the sword from the stone. Actually, it was a crowbar imbedded solidly in a barrel of cement, but never mind, it was the same thing.

Zac remembered the way Merlin had first scared him into listening with tricks involving a disappearing Bengal tiger and some other wild tricks in the park.

At first, of course, he had thought the old man was crazy. He wasn't the famous magician, but good ol' friendly Max Merlin, who ran the gas station. Well, maybe not so friendly. Grumpy, actually, most of the time. But never cruel or petty. Just didn't seem to care much for the modern world.

"Too many people," Max would mutter. "Not enough human beings."

Good ol' Max Merlin. The kindly garage owner with the rich tastes; the dungaree-clad mechanic with the secret room. Oh, that Crystal Room, Zac moaned. All those retorts and stoppered bottles; that huge book, the biggest book Zac had ever seen, with all those spells; the racks and archaic devices.

Merlin's laboratory. Merlin's secret lair.

Zac shrank into a tighter shape in the darkness as his pursuer came back down the street. He stopped only a few feet away and his voice was low, but penetrating. "You listen and you listen good, kid. You go to the cops and you'll never see your girl-friend again. Not alive, anyway. This ain't no threat, punk, this is the choice you have. Not choices. Choice. Cops equal one still high school sweetie."

The man turned and strode down the street. Zac slipped out on the sidewalk side and, crouching low, went quickly down toward the cable anchorage. He stopped as he heard the man talk to the one who was holding Julie.

"Get her inside. Charlie and Lefty must have got all them electric eyes fixed by now."

"Yeah, okay," the man said. "Listen, Gino, just how good are these guys?"

"They did the Wells Fargo job last month. Slick as anything. And the Parsons job down in Phoenix three, four months back. Security all over the place, but they got some way of feeding back the signal and everything looks just dandy. Only time it shows is a blip when they clip in and when they pull out. Lotsa things cause blips. Nothing to worry about."

"Yeah, okay, I just—hey!" Julie had kicked the man in the shins and tried to wiggle loose.

"Heh—!" she began but his hand went over her mouth again.

"Get her inside, Bozo," Gino ordered.

At that moment Zac stood up, preparing himself for the intense mental effort that was needed for even the smallest feat of magic.

Not that he knew much. He was, after all, only an apprentice. A *new* apprentice. Merlin made it look so easy, as though he just willed it and it happened. Not all that easy. It couldn't be that easy, as Merlin had explained. "We all get irritated," Merlin had told him. "We say things, do things, out of annoyance, anger, fear. We don't mean them, maybe, but when you are playing around with magic, you must be careful!"

So Zac rose to blast the bad guys in the only spell he had learned that seemed to apply. The Spell of Incompetence was the only one he could think of . . . and he thought it . . . just as Gino saw him and fired.

Plunk!

The silenced slug buried itself deeply into the radiator of the 1979 Buick Riviera in front of Zac. He forgot all about the Spell of Incompetence.

Whannnng!

A second slug ricocheted off the top of the grille, spinning nastily away into the gloom. Zac stood, staring. Guns made such immense flares at night. He'd seen nothing like that on the tube. The whole street seemed to light up for a fraction of a second.

I'm being shot at, he thought with a kind of distracted amazement. Me, Zachary Rogers, is a target.

"Yipe!" Zac said and hunched down behind the car. What to do, what to do?

He'll come close to finish me off and I'll jump up in the air and give him my best Bruce Lee kick, complete with wild yell and everything.

But Zachary Rogers didn't know how to do that sort of thing.

I'll . . . I'll slide under the car and when he gets close, I'll grab his leg and . . . and get shot. All he has to do is point and squeeze.

He could run.

The thought came to him, shamefaced and ugly. Run. Run away from danger and leave Julie to—

No!

Live again another day . . .

No!

Go get the cops and . . . get Julie killed.

Use magic. Think of something. What has Merlin taught me?

How To Keep Off Stinging Insects. How to Make Butterflies Congregate. How to Make Dogs Stop Barking at Night. How to Decaffeinate Coffee Already Made. Removing Bunions, Splinters, and Warts. The Spell of Minor Incompetence.

Baby spells. Lessons to be learned, like the ABCs of magic. They were practice lessons, suitable for a beginner. Zac groaned, then clamped a hand over his mouth.

Quickly, he scurried along, away from the approaching gun-bearing thug. These guys mean business! Two cars back, he crouched behind a blue 1970 Chevy Impala with a dent in the driver's side. He kicked a strip of bent chrome lying in the gutter and an idea formed in his mind.

Scooping up the strip, he tossed it high in the air, toward the opposite side of the street. He heard the thug swear and the thump of a silenced slug, then the whining of a ricocheting bullet.

"Come on, Gino," Bozo said hoarsely. "The kid's too scared to do anything."

"And he'll know his girl will get hers if he does do anything," Gino growled.

"Come on," Bozo urged. "Pinky'll have the tape of the ransom demand at the radio station by now."

"Ransom?" Zac said aloud, without thinking. Ransom? Not for Julie ... it was too soon, all accidental.

Zac looked overhead, then down at the anchorage. Of course. Pay up or get blown up. Destroy the cables and the bridge would fall.

He heard a soft metallic slam and peeked around to see that the anchorage door was shut. No Julie. He was alone on the street and his girl was a prisoner and there was very little he could do about it.

But Max Merlin could.

No cops—okay. But Max Merlin was no cop.

He raced toward his parked car farther up the street. Thoughts were running frantically through his head. Do I have time? Can Merlin take them? How much time do I have?

His mouth formed a determined line. The answers to the questions made no difference. Julie had to be rescued and the Oakland–Bay Bridge had to be saved.

He started running.

Chapter Two

The garage was closed, as Zac knew it would be. He didn't even slow up as he sped past the station toward Merlin's Victorian house a short distance away. Not much time, not much time!

Zac skidded Merlin's old car to a stop in front of the bay-windowed facade on the slanted street. He jammed on the handbrake and left the car double-parked. As usual, everywhere in San Francisco, parking was at a premium. Zac often joked with his friend Leo about parking places being hereditary.

Jumping out, Zac shot across the sidewalk and up the steps in long-legged bounds. He stabbed at the doorbell, then stabbed again and again. He thought he heard a growl from within and then a hollow, poofing sound.

"Mister Merlin! Max! It's me, Zac!"

The excited boy heard footsteps and then the door was unlatched and swung inward to reveal a glowering Max Merlin in a velvet smoking jacket with gold braid piping and black tuxedo trousers.

"What is it, Zachary Rogers?" Merlin said in an icy tone.

At other times, Zac would have cringed at the tone of angry impatience, but this time it was different. Without waiting for an invitation he stormed in, talking rapidly.

"They've got Julie, Max! Crooks, they've got Julie and they'll kill her if we call the police and they fired shots at me and they're planning to blow up the bridge and I'm afraid Julie will be killed and—"

"Wait a minute, wait a minute," Merlin said.

"—they are pretty desperate guys and one is Gino, the other Bozo, but there are more inside and—"

"Zac . . ."

"—they have explosives and a ransom note is going to a radio station and—"

Merlin clamped his jaws together in annoyance. Zac suddenly found he had no voice. "Urk . . . awk . . . urr . . ."

"Now," Merlin said softly. "What is this about?"

Zac found his voice. He backed up and told it as he remembered it, except for the part about thinking about running. "So here I am," Zac said. Then he looked around.

Candles. The dining room table was tastefully laid out with an embroidered white cloth. Silver dragon candlesticks. A polished Sumerian urn filled with caviar. A Tiffany ice bucket with an opened magnum of Dom Perignon '71. Two glasses, both partially empty. Two plates, two sets of elaborate silver. A big covered silver dish. Aroma. Scents. Flowers on the mantel.

"Oh, did I disturb anything?" Zac asked.

Merlin made a face. "No, not really. An old friend dropped by."

"Oh, I'm sorry, I . . ."

"Never mind," the old man sighed. "She's gone now."

"Good," Zac said. "Then let's go."

"Wait a minute," Merlin said, "let me think."

Zac paced restlessly, glancing at the short, pudgy, gray-haired man with impatience.

"Yes, I remember when they poured the anchorage back in the thirties," Merlin said. "Huge block of steel and concrete, anchored to the bedrock."

"Yeah, yeah, that's it, let's go."

"Zac, you must learn not to be impatient. Impatience can spoil anything, given the chance. Proceed slowly with haste and all that."

"Yeah, but every minute that Julie—"

"Come on, Zac." The old magician walked toward the carved Victorian door in one wall of his living room. Zac followed eagerly. If anyone who did not have "the touch" opened the doors, all they would find would be a small closet filled with cut glass, fine china, damask, and linen. But if someone who was "an adept" opened the door, what they found was vastly different.

Merlin reached for the polished brass doorknob and twisted. Zac sucked in air. He had never gotten used to the sight.

Beyond the oak frame was space.

The void of eternal night. Stars and galaxies turned in slow grace. Within seconds of watching, uncounted eons of time seemed to pass. Pinwheel galaxies seemed to rotate in inexorable strength. Stars, born of dust and gravity, lived and died. Worlds grew from specks into globes of beauty. Life was born from mud and lightning. Civilizations rose and fell.

Zac was not certain what he was looking at and never had been sure. Was this the story of the universe? Was this the past or the future? Or both? Or something else entirely, some kind of special effect whipped up by the smart guys at Industrial Light and Magic, who did the effects for *Star Wars*?

"Come on, Zac," Merlin said.

They went up the curving white stairway that jutted out into space from the living room door, up to the crystal door at the top.

And into Merlin's Crystal Room, the secret room, the heart of Merlin's studies.

It was white and huge, filled with things: racks and carved tables with dragon's-foot legs, stoppered bottles, and ancient books; jars filled with obscure potions and the spices of a magician's skills. In the center of the main room was a high stand and on it the great, red, leather-bound book simply stamped in gold, *Merlin*.

"Um," Merlin said, lifting the heavy cover of the great book of spells, arcana, and esoteric knowlege. "Um," he said again as he rattled through the stiff parchment sheets. "Um," he said with satisfaction as he found the proper page.

"Just to refresh my mind," Merlin said. Then he turned to a nearby stand, whose sole burden was a gleaming crystal globe in an ornately carved stand. This was Merlin's Eye, the all-seeing orb by which he could peer into secret places.

"Let's just see what these ruffians are up to," Merlin said. The milkiness of the globe cleared. Zac moved to get a reflection from a candelabra out of the way.

It was the inside of the cable anchorage, a high room which vaguely reminded Zac of either an unfinished cathedral or a Universal Pictures horror set. Sheer gray concrete walls, unadorned, rose steeply. A few bare electric fixtures were set in the wall. The main entrance to the raised platform running the width of the room was about twenty feet long. On either end of the platform, which had an iron pipe railing, were two openings.

The big room was just a little wider than

the width of the multilane bridge. Zac realized the side rooms must be where the foot-thick steel cables came in, to bury themselves in the concrete mountain.

And in the middle, tied to the iron railing, was Julie.

"There's Julie!" Zac exclaimed, unnecessarily.

Merlin didn't respond. He was studying the four thugs who were in the wide, tall, but shallow room.

One was backing out of the right-hand cable room, unraveling wires behind him, spinning them from a reel. He put the reel down next to an open suitcase and bent over it. The view in the crystal sphere changed as it zoomed in on the suitcase.

Within were several large batteries, a timing device, and a .38 Special revolver. Zac and Merlin saw the crook fasten the wires to the timing device, which already was hooked up to the explosives in the other side room.

"Uh-oh," Zac said. "They're all hooked up."

"Let's see if we can do something about that," Merlin said. The view in the crystal ball pulled back to give a fuller view.

Suddenly, a wind ruffled Julie's dress and blew the cap off Gino who was still carrying a gun. "Hey!" the crook yelled, looking at the door.

"Must be the air-conditioning," Lefty said, looking up from the suitcase.

Merlin's face grimaced. "I'm getting interference," he said. He stared again at the scene in the anchorage.

Julie yelped as a bat zoomed past her face. Another and another and another came plunging out of the shadows and skimmed close to the captive girl, then flew by the faces of the startled crooks. "Hey! Hey!" Bozo yelled, waving his hands.

"They won't hurt you," Gino growled, looking up into the "belfry" of the high, dark room, gun in hand.

The bats fluttered up and it was silent again.

Merlin growled angrily, "It must be all that thick concrete and steel. I was aiming for a plague of spiders to drop on them."

"Urk!" Zac said, squirming.

"I'll try again," the old sorcerer said, frowning in concentration.

"Hey, Gino," Charlie said, "you dint tell me it was going to be this cold!" The crook hugged himself, his breath beginning to appear in a fine mist.

"You musta gimmicked the air conditioner somehow," Gino grumbled to Lefty, who shrugged.

"How'd I know? These are the original plans I'm working from, boss. Nineteen-thirty-six update is the latest. They didn't even have air-conditioning then, did they?"

"I dunno, but it's getting cold in here!" Gino said. He stared at his frosty breath with some surprise.

"It's not working," Merlin grumbled.

"Try, uh, try to immobilize them," Zac suggested.

Merlin gave him a withering look. "Maybe in person, but not through all that concrete and metal."

"Then, uh, then ruin their detonation thing!"

Merlin rolled his eyes upward. "Great Arthur, Zac, I'm getting enough static now! I might accidently start that thing going! I can't take that chance."

"Then, uh—"

"Shush," the old magician said, pursing his lips and looking off into the great inner distance of his mind.

"I am reminded of a time with Sir Gawain," the old man said musingly. "Had a great villain of a fellow penned up in a castle. Had some sort of princess there, too, we thought, but it turned out later to be a country wench with good skin. But the good knights simply couldn't get in. Dreadfully well-built place. Naturally, they called up the heavy artillery."

"Artillery?" Zac said in surprise.

"Figure of speech. Artillery hadn't been invented yet. Me, that's who they brought up. They wanted me to spirit the whole of Gawain's forces right inside. Just like that. Never do they think what it costs *me*! 'Just put us inside, good wizard, and we shall do the rest,' Gawain said. That egotistical—"

"Gawain, that's Prince Valiant's friend," Zac said, again earning a withering look from Merlin.

"Valiant is pure fiction and there were times . . . oh, were there ever times when I wished that romantic fool, Gawain, the Green Knight, was fiction too."

"But what happened?"

"I was captured."

"Captured!"

"Don't look so stricken, my dear boy. You have to get close to do the best sort of magic, you know. Look them in the eye, that sort of thing. Oh, it will usually work at a distance, of course, but you can't know the details."

"Details?"

"Will you stop repeating everything I say? Yes, captured. I was in no real danger, of course, but I had to see things up close. I recall a time in the eighteenth century. Marie was queen of France then. Lovely girl."

"Marie?"

"Marie Antoinette, the wife of Louis the Sixteenth, you historical numbskull. The French hated her, thought she was an Austrian spy, you know. Probably did more to bring about the French Revolution than anyone. Headstrong as . . . well, I'm wandering."

"Boy, are you . . ."

"There was this plot and . . . well, I knew the queen well . . . very well . . ." A nostalgic smile came over Merlin's face. "Uh, well, yes. There was this court intrigue, you see. A plot to frame her with an Austrian lover, catch 'em at it, you know. Dreadful consequences . . ."

"*Merlin!*"

"My job was to switch it all around. She knew about it, of course. She had her own spies everywhere. Knew about me, too. Used to blackmail me into doing the most . . . well, um . . . never mind that. Needless to say that I, at a distance, mind you, had to magic that Austrian out of there in a hurry. No one told me he was wearing armor. I couldn't hold him. He fell, broke half the bones in his body. Lucky to be alive. I made it up to him afterwards, of course, but if I had been up close I'd have seen the armor, I know that."

"Merlin, Julie—"

"So I had myself captured. Wandering minstrel sort of thing. They took me, thinking I could give them all the latest information on Gawain's force. Gawain was never a siege man, of course. Sieges are not romantic. Dull, really. Dull with bits of terror. Not his cup of tea at all. All dash and flourish, that lad. Oh, handsome, yes. Absolutely first-rate in a one-on-one. But a poor administrator. Impatient. Wanted things over in a big hurry."

"Julie is—"

"So I got in, looked around, spotted the whole thing right off. Postern gate. Easy as pie. Put the guards to sleep, in comes Gawain, and the whole thing was over before the cock crowed."

"Merlin, I—"

"You want your Julie rescued, of course. Nothing to it. Just get me into that anchorage castle and all will be done."

"I hope so," breathed Zac.

"Well, what are you waiting there for?" Merlin said from the Crystal Door. "Let us be off!"

Chapter Three

It was very dark around the base of the
bridge when Zac and Merlin crept up. They
could hear the noise of late traffic overhead
and see the flash of headlights on the steel.
The lower-level traffic was all one way, east
toward Oakland and Berkeley. They didn't
have the view that the westbound, toward-
San Francisco traffic had on the top level of
the two-tiered bridge.

"I don't see any outside guard," Zac whispered.

"Might be in one of the cars parked along
here," Merlin said.

Blink, blink, blink, blink, blink, blink. All
the interior lights came on in each car and

truck cab on the street. They were all empty, as far as Zac could see. The lights all blinked out and the street seemed darker than ever.

"Let's get closer," Merlin said. "Maybe we can hear something."

"Door's pretty thick. Steel or something, I think. Maybe bronze," Zac said.

"There's a way to open any door," Merlin said cryptically.

They walked quietly along the street, eyeing every shadow and car. Zac saw the water from the ruined radiator running sluggishly in the street, a thin trickle glistening in the glow from a distant street light. The owner's going to be very angry, the boy thought.

Merlin went right up to the door and pressed his ear against the almost featureless iron door set back into the thick wall. He held up a hand for silence, then after a moment he straightened up.

"They are not much on conversation." The old man looked up and down the deserted street. "All right, I think it's time for my act."

"Act?"

"You're doing that again, Zachary. Stop it."

"Stop what?"

"That. Repeating everything I say."

"*I* repeat everything you say?"

Merlin's eyes rolled up again, then he waved the boy back. "Get in those shadows. I don't want them to see you."

"But what will I do if you get inside?"

"Not if . . . when. You just sit still. I'll take care of everything."

Uncertain, but obedient, Zac pressed himself back into the shadows. He was quite excited. This was field training that Merlin said wouldn't be coming along for some time yet.

He saw Merlin walk into a patch of shadow and out the other side. Only it wasn't Merlin who came out. Zac blinked in astonishment. He still wasn't used to Merlin's quiet ways.

What came out of the shadows was a derelict. A bum in a coat two sizes too big, tattered and stained. His shoes didn't match. He was unshaven and rumpled, with red-rimmed eyes and a suspicious paper sack bulging from one sagging coat pocket.

Zac saw Merlin go toward the steel door. Behind that door was Julie Potter. Zac Rodgers wondered what was happening to her.

And what, if anything, he should do now.

Julie stood as straight-backed as she could, chin up, a noble and brave expression on her face. She hoped her trembling did not show. It never did any good to show people you were scared, she knew.

Even when none of the four thugs were in sight, she practiced withering looks and killing stares. They'd never break *her*!

The chilling cold had gone, but the huge concrete vault was still cold enough. She looked around, and then up, at the tall room where it deepened into shadows.

He'd come, she knew it. He always had.

The trouble was, Julie wasn't certain just who he would be. Errol Flynn would be just about perfect, she thought. Poised up on the balcony that she just knew had to be up there in the shadows somewhere. His forest-green suit, his tights, his quiver of arrows, the bow strung across his back.

Laughing.

Always that light, mocking laugh.

"So those are your best bowmen, Prince

Gino?" The laugh. "Better for skewering marshmallows, methinks, milord."

Tink! Whinng! Thunk!

The arrows from Gino's thugs would ping off the concrete. Errol would duck, coming up with fierce expression and a strung bow. *Whang!* One of Prince Gino's brawny thugs would get it. Another arrow would just miss Gino himself, saved for the swordfight at the end.

Thunk! A Sherwood arrow into Lefty's suitcase of gimmicks. A shower of sparks and the threat would be over.

Errol would swing down on a tasseled rope. One cut of his sword and she would be free. He'd start a duel with Lefty, and Charlie would run in from the back. But she'd save him, breaking a vase over his head.

Hmm, no vase. Well, something.

Then the long fight. Great, stark shadows up the walls from the torchlights. The metallic crash and rasp of steel, the taunts and jeers. Oh, for a big, thick candle to cut through!

"Hey, Gino, how long before Pinky gets here, huh?"

Gino looked at his wristwatch. "Take it

easy, Charlie. Lotsa time, yet." The big man walked back and forth impatiently. He glanced up at Julie but she sniffed and looked away.

Gino muttered something and Bozo said, "Whatcha say?"

"Nothing," Gino answered sharply.

"No, boss, ya said sumpin'. About the chick, I mean."

"Never mind about the chick. Stay by the door. Listen."

"Yeah, okay, boss. Gotcha." The thug shuffled back against the recessed door and tilted his head. He caught Julie looking at him and he winked.

Her head snapped away disdainfully. Maybe Tyrone Power. He'd come, tall and curly-headed, with a breastplate and leggings. Or like Zorro, maybe. A swirl of black cape, a mask, scratching a "Z" in the concrete, his sword rasping across the naked cement wall.

"*Señores* ..." A bow, the dark cape swirling. The deep, intense voice, the dark, intense eyes. Oh, and music. Erich Wolfgang Korngold, just like in the Errol Flynn movies. The *Star Wars* score was like a Korngold composition.

The full orchestra scored the scene in her mind, the swoops and swirls keyed to the jumps and swordplay. Bozo was a bit fat—he'd make a good sergeant for comic relief. A "Z" across his uniform trousers, his eyes staring at the sword point at his throat.

"You double-checked everything?" Gino demanded.

"Everything, Gino, honest," Lefty said wearily. "New batteries, everything. Stop worrying. If we gotta blow it, it'll blow."

"You men are fools," snapped Julie. "If they don't pay you the ransom, why blow it up? You gain nothing."

Gino sighed. "Shuddup," he growled.

"They'll have this place surrounded—"

"*Shuddup!*

Charlie wandered over near Julie and leaned against the iron railing. "Professional reputation, darlin'. A man's got to do what he says or who will believe him next time, huh? If every time some hood says he's gonna do somethin' and doesn't, it makes it bad on alla us. Who'll believe us, huh?"

"You're mad!" Julie said.

Charlie grinned. "You forgot the part about not getting away with it. I always liked that part. Those goody-goody dames were always so blah, except during scenes like that. *'Take your hands off me!'*" Charlie laughed throatily after saying the last line in a shrill, feminine voice. "I wish those screenwriters would get outta the house sometimes, you know what I mean? Crime *does* pay, don't they know that?" He leaned toward Julie, who shrank back as far as her bonds would let her. "Why don't they know that, huh? Everyone in the street knows it. You get off 'cause you're young or it's the first time you got caught. Or because you're crazy or because of some technicality. Only a teeny-tiny percentage gets caught and only a few of those get sent up."

Charlie laughed nastily. "Ain't that a kick? Oh, we'll get away with it, honey. We got things all figured out." Chuckling, he walked away, leaving a frightened Julie staring after him.

I bet Sean Connery could do it, she thought. Tuxedo, flower in his lapel, quip on his tongue. "Good evening, gentlemen. Up to your usual no good, I see. Ah, Mister Big. That's a nine-millimeter Bertinelli, isn't it? Customized, of course. I prefer the Bretta. No wine? How uncivilized of you. Ah, Miss Potter. You are looking well."

"Listen, you," Gino would growl, the automatic in his hairy paw aimed straight at Connery's heart. "Getcha mitts in the air."

"Certainly, old chap."

"Lefty, wire 'em up."

"Right, boss."

The explosive wire tying their wrists together, hands over their heads, back to back. His scent was disarming, exciting. Three minutes to go. The biggest explosion in San Francisco history. The bridge crumpling, sending hundreds of people to their deaths, trapped in cars splashing into the bay.

"A last cigarette, old man?"

Lefty would look to Gino for confirmation. A curt nod. What could this fellow do, after all?

"Inside the jacket pocket ... that's a good lad .."

Lefty would scream, jerking his hand out, the cigarette case clinging to his fingers like an outraged clam. Connery would kick. Swing. Use his feet to pick up Lefty's snippers. Toss them deftly up to his hands.

Snip. Snip. Freedom. *Whack! Thud! Socko!*

Thunk, thunk.

"Whuzzat?" Bozo said, his eyes opening wide.

"Someone's at the door, stupid," Gino snapped.

"Gotta be Pinky," Charlie said, but his gun slid into his hand anyway.

Thunk, thunk, thunk.

"A little early," Gino said. But he gestured to Bozo. "Go ahead." His gun, still with its long, thick silencer, snaked out of his jacket.

Click. Clang. Squeak. The door swung back. A figure stood swaying on the doorstep.

"Hiya," Merlin said. "I saw yer light on. Wanta drink?"

"Whew!" Bozo said, waving his hand. "Beat it, old man."

Merlin took a couple of unsteady steps into the room, looking around. "Hey, this is a pretty crummy joint. You guys gotta dress it up a little if you want my business." He hiccuped. "Hang a fishnet over there, maybe a coupla them blowfish up there. Oh, hi, there, miss."

"Get outta here, ya bum," Bozo said, reaching for Merlin's arm. He missed and staggered past, cracking his head painfully on the edge of the open steel door. "Owww!"

The old bum paid the stumbling crook no

attention at all. He grinned foolishly and took a few steps into the room, looking around in bleary-eyed astonishment. "You guys need chairs in here, I tell ya. Tables. Those teardrop-shaped glasses with the netting and the candles inside. Got a name for it yet?" He looked up into Lefty's face as the man came for him, grabbing his arm.

"We'll think of one," Lefty said, turning the bum around. Only they kept going. All the way around, with Lefty losing his balance and tripping over his own feet. He fell hard, smacking loudly onto the uncarpeted concrete floor and not moving.

"How about Troll House?" the staggering bum said. "You know, under the bridge and all. Troll Room? Troll Bowl?" He hiccuped loudly. "Excuse me," he said with dignity, then did it again.

Lefty looked at Gino and they both moved in toward the whiskery bum. Julie—who had recognized Merlin, the garage owner, in his Barbary Coast disguise—saw Gino raise his silenced automatic. "Look out!" she screamed.

But Merlin thought she meant the villainous-looking Lefty, who was starting a roundhouse punch. Lefty's shoelaces untied themselves and leaped across to twist around each other. Lefty let out a curse as he swung. His whole balance was thrown off and he went yelling off to the left, thumping into the edge of the platform and cracking his head against the concrete.

Merlin never heard Julie's second scream. The thick metal tube of the silencer slammed down over his ear.

The last thing Max Merlin remembered was, "It *is* like falling into a hole, just like all those detective-story writers said—"

Zac stared at the closed steel door.

Nothing. Nothing at all. He expected it to open soon, but it had been over five minutes since Merlin had gone in, and the door was still firmly closed.

Zac edged closer, creeping along the sheer face of the cement cliff. There was a long freighter edging through the waters of the bay. A trace of fog was creeping in from the Golden Gate. The offramps from the bridge traffic were not far off, yet they might as well have been a million miles away.

Zac bent and pressed an ear against the

steel. Nothing. He pressed his ear tighter against the cold metal. Nothing.

What was going on?

They used some of Lefty's surplus wire to fasten the old bum's wrists to the railing. He hung limply, below and to the left of where Julie was lashed to the railing on the platform between the two rooms.

Julie wanted to call out to the old man, to wake him up, but she also wanted to keep his identity a secret. Why the nice old man from the garage had disguised himself as a bum was beyond her. It had to be some kind of trick.

Or was nice old Max Merlin a secret drinker?

Did he have a secret second life, roaming the alleys of North Beach?

Julie stood up straight. No, she'd have to get herself out of this. She had spunk. She had grit, by golly. She was definitely not one of those old-fashioned heroines who cringed back against the wall and screamed uselessly. No, not her. *She'd* get herself and poor drunken old Mr. Merlin out of this pickle. Or die trying.

She gulped. Or die trying. Oh, dear, she thought. This *is* the real thing, isn't it? Those are real gangsters or terrorists or whatever they are. That's real explosive. This is real wire, tying me up here.

They mean it.

They aren't kidding.

"Mister . . . mister? Wake up, mister!"

Max Merlin felt pain in his head and pain in his wrists. He opened his eyes reluctantly and saw the blurred, slightly tilted room. Modern architecture—bah! The least a person could expect were floors that are flat.

Ah, well, on with the rescue. Let's see now, a good spell for immobility, just freeze these bad guys in their tracks.

What was that spell? Oh, yes, Number 3,156.

Darn, faded out. Wait a minute. Visualize the page. That's it, the one with the wine stain left by Morgan Le Fey when he caught her going through his treasured volume.

It goes like this, I think, he thought.

Across the bay, in the stadium, Galen Tripp was running hard. The fifty, the forty, the thirty. Over his shoulder he could see the quarterback snap back his arm and rifle the pigskin right to where he was going to be in just a few seconds.

Everything slowed. The ball was wobbling. He sidestepped Pelz the Punisher and leaped skyward. . . .

His hands were out, spread and ready, only he couldn't move. He fell heavily, arms still stretched out, falling atop Pelz the Punisher, who was also frozen. They toppled like tin soldiers cast aside by a petulant child.

The ball bounced erratically down to the ten-yard line and rolled to a stop in absolute silence.

No one in the stands moved.

They couldn't.

Chapter Four

Merlin's spell, cast in the general direction of Gino, had accidently skipped across San Francisco Bay, to paralyze the football fans at the Oakland A's stadium, where Galen Tripp lay with his face in the grass, wondering if he'd played one too many games.

But that was not all. In the wooded Oakland hills a young female writer sitting poised at her typewriter, fingers ready to plunge down upon the keys for that final, perfect phrase . . . stayed poised.

The driver of a small foreign car sat at a stoplight while it turned green, then red, then green again while an impatient driver in an 18-wheeler behind him honked. And honked. And honked.

Fourteen families sat watching television. And watched. And watched.

Unk!

Merlin's vision blurred, his mind took a right-hand turn. Galen Tripp collapsed from his frozen position. The umpire's whistle blew. "Incomplete!" The crowd blinked and decided not to mention it to each other—it had to be some strange flu coming on. Three hundred and sixteen football fans made vows to see their doctors as soon as possible.

The female writer's fingers decided on the keys to tap "Lady Caroline txieo dj½q;w sjsuwkx." Then she stared at the keys awhile.

The driver in the foreign car wrenched it into gear, shooting across against the red light, ducked into a parking place, and sat quivering for thirteen minutes.

And Zachary Rodgers screwed up his face, pressed his ear against the steel door, and tried in vain to hear something.

Inside, Max Merlin looked around in bewilderment. "Why is there fog in here?" he muttered.

"Eh?" Gino said, grumpily, looking up from his watch.

"Don't you tell them a thing, Mister Merlin," Julie said firmly to the confused wizard.

"You know this bum?" Bozo asked.

Julie stammered. "I ... uh ... I've, uh, seen him around. Yes, he's a regular. Sleeps in Kurland's doorway. In summers."

Merlin looked up at her. "Do I know you? You aren't one of Gawain's friends, are you?"

Oh, thought Julie, pretending not to know me. Must be part of a plan. "No, I ..." She couldn't think of anything to say. These are desperate men, she thought. One tiny slip and they'll pounce on me. Torture the truth out of me.

She frowned, tugging futilely at the wire. This is getting annoying, she thought. It's about time I was rescued. Enough, already!

Merlin looked around at the concrete walls. "Dreary palace. Needs some color. A Gobelin tapestry or two. Suit of armor there."

Gino looked at Bozo and made a finger-whirling motion near his temple. Lefty looked at the bewhiskered old man and decided to stop drinking.

"Hey, Charlie," Lefty said. "Whatcha gonna do with your part of the money?"

"Charlie will blow it," Gino said, knowingly.

"Aw, c'mon, Gino. There's this great

little Italian restaurant down in Palo Alto. A cousin of mine owns it. Looking for a partner."

"You're gonna *work*?" Lefty said in amazement. "Man, your share of this will be two million bucks!"

Charlie shook his head. "You gotta be practical, Lefty. You gonna live down in Argentina or someplace, huh? You speak the language? No TV, no good American beer, no Monday Night Football, huh?" He shook his head. "Naw, ya gotta be practical. The IRS will be all over you like syrup on pancakes. How you gonna prove you got any money legitimately, huh? You get a nice cash business, you feed the bread in, you pay your taxes, and—"

"Pay taxes?" Lefty said in surprise.

"Taxes?" Bozo said.

"To the government?" Gino said.

Charlie shrugged. "I know I'm talking dirty, guys, but if ya don't..." He shrugged again.

Bozo sat down on the concrete stops dejectedly. "That's a terrible thought."

Two million dollars each! Julie thought. With these four and the one out delivering the ransom note, that's five. Ten million dollars. Then she thought about the replacement cost of the bridge—and the buildings under it—not even to mention any lives lost. Ten million was really a modest request, all things considered.

Julie gave the crooks a second appraising look. They don't look like modest people, she thought. Maybe they are just stupid, or can't think higher than a million per finger.

I should be able to outwit them, she thought.

If I can just figure out how.

She looked again at Mr. Merlin, hiding her look in a sly, sideways glance. He seemed confused, even drunk. Is that a trick? she wondered. She saw him stare around him, muttering to himself. She tried to get closer to hear, but couldn't.

"Is Arthur angry with me?" Merlin said to the nearest of the crooks, Lefty.

"Huh?" Lefty said brightly.

"Arthur," Merlin said.

"My name's Lefty," Lefty said. "Well, it's really Lionel," he said diffidently.

"Ah, Sir Lyonel!" Merlin said, smiling.

"No, just, uh, Lionel," Lefty said, looking around. "You look, old man, uh, cool it with the Lionel, huh? That's why I don't mind the Lefty, see?"

"And Sir Lancelot? Is he well?" Merlin

peered closely at Lefty. "Your pardon, sir, but you don't look like the noble knight. Your uncle, the brave Lancelot..." Merlin paused, as if lost in thought, his words wandering away.

Merlin looked around and saw Julie looking at him. "Ah, milady. Have you..." Again his words died as he saw the wire on her wrists. He blinked, focusing hard, trying to understand.

"Why, these ruffians have—!" Merlin straightened, a scowl darkening his face. It began to rain in the cable anchorage.

"What the—!" Gino jumped into the recessed doorway. The water came down in torrents, falling out of the darkness.

"Boss, we musta busted a pipe or set off some kinda sprinkler system up there!"

Julie, almost immediately drenched, tugged at the wire holding her to the iron railing, but it was of no avail. She saw Max Merlin staring up into the falling water as if bewildered. Poor old man! she thought.

"That's not right," Merlin mumbled. "Got to get it *right*," he said. He swayed a little, held erect by the wire around his wrists attached to the iron pipe railing.

A lightning bolt crackled through the rain, striking the iron door just behind Gino. He screamed and fell forward, splashing into the inch of water already on the floor.

Outside, Zac Rodgers had been thrown across the sidewalk and sat in the gutter, a ringing in his ears and a kettledrum in his head.

"If I hadn't looked up at that passing car—" he said with a shiver, realizing his head had been only inches from death.

Gino picked himself up and bellowed at his men. "Lefty! Bozo! Find that shutoff valve! Charlie, guard the door!"

A chorus of "Yeah, boss" was heard.

Then the rain stopped.

Dead. Not a final drip, nothing; it just stopped. The silence was ominous. Gino splashed around, soaking his shoes and cursing.

Max Merlin frowned at him, focusing his blurry vision upon the thug, summoning up from the depths of his experience a terrible and sudden affliction—

—and missed.

Three blocks to the northeast a waiter named Patrick was just getting home. He opened his apartment door and found the floor covered with frogs.

They started croaking.

He slammed the door and stood shaking against the wall. "I won't empty the customers' champagne glasses anymore," he swore. "I won't sneak any of André's cooking sherry." Armed with the new truth, he put his key in the lock and turned the knob.

Ribbit.

Ribbit, ribbit, ribbit, RIBBIT!

In a straight line, one block farther northeast, a retired couple stared at their local newscaster on the television screen. "Why is that nice man wearing a frog mask?" she asked.

"I don't think it's a mask," offered her husband.

Near Fisherman's Wharf, a heating contractor, on vacation from Fond du Lac, Wisconsin, ran out of the motel bathroom and slammed the door behind him, throwing his weight against it.

"What in heaven is the matter?" the woman asked.

"Call the cops! It's Moby Frog!"

At Alioto's, a diner looked at the just-served plate, then at his busy waiter. "I know I ordered frog's legs, but I thought they would be cooked."

The waiter looked at the plate.

Ribbit!

On the Golden Gate Bridge one of the toll-takers stared after a departing Ford pickup. "What's the matter?" the tollperson to the south asked. "Something from the hot-sheet?"

"No, no . . ." the first tollperson responded, swinging back to accept the money from the next car. It just *couldn't* have been a frog driving that pickup.

But the license plate did say RIBBIT.

Max Merlin shook his head to clear it. Something was wrong. Sir Lyonel just didn't look like Sir Lyonel. This was a most peculiar castle. Not the dungeon but yet . . . yet Lady Julie was also a prisoner. What had he done wrong?

Had Arthur found out about the little dalliance with the Cornish serving maid? Or the potion he had made up for Sir Pelleas? No, that wasn't right . . .

"My head hurts," Merlin grumbled irascibly.

"Shuddup, old man," Gino said, trying to see up into the higher regions of the room.

Julie was looking up, too. Had the sudden

start and stop of the sprinkler system been some sort of signal?

She shook herself, still soaking wet. Not a good way to be rescued, she thought. Artistically disheveled, of course, but soaking wet, with hair that looked like rat tails. What will Zac think when he comes to—

"Oh," she said softly. Zac. Zachary Rogers.

She blushed slightly, remembering some of her dreams. I'm so immature! she chastised herself. He's just a kid, like me.

But cute.

A little less of a stumbling idiot than most of the boys my age, she told herself. If only a girl could have a boyfriend her own age, sharing the same interests, who wasn't a complete nerd. Older men are so cool and sophisticated, but they are, after all, older. They don't know any of the members of Raw Material or even the Mutant Horde.

How *anyone* could not know who was in the Mutant Horde, their whole lives, and what they did when they weren't recording was a mystery to Julie. But none of the older men she knew—as old as twenty-eight or thirty—knew a thing about the good new music, or the new groups, or even *cared*. What *did* they care about, she wondered.

Zac did, though. Or did he? Julie frowned.

He'd been so straight arrow lately, what with his school work, his new job, and all that reading he was doing. It was only a few days since she asked him if he was going to the concert or not and he had said, "What concert?"

Boys! Maybe they weren't as excited about Harry Barker as girls were, but he ought to know Raw Material was in town! Really! Maybe Zac wasn't the rescuing sort . . .

But if he was . . .

How would he do it, Julie wondered.

Sometimes he is a klutz. He'd probably find some secret way in, some sneaky way in, and knock over something and get himself shot.

Julie shivered. Bad thoughts! No, no, he'd find a way in, not trip over something, and . . .

. . . and . . .

. . . and what?

What could a sixteen-year-old kid do with four big, strong thugs? she asked herself. Her dream collapsed. Forget it. No daring rescue by Zachary Rogers.

Julie went back to trying to imagine how some other dashing hero would rescue her. Errol Flynn, Douglas Fairbanks, Tyrone Power were all dead and she'd heard that

Sean Connery was off in England making a movie. Who else was there?

She shook her head sadly. Fine situation. No heroes anymore, no real heroes, the kind you can believe in, can believe could rescue a girl . . .

Oh, when Connery came to rescue Bergen in *The Wind and the Lion* . . .

Julie sighed, her shoulders slumping.

Zac stood up in the street, the ringing in his ears slowly going away, like a band marching up the street. He saw water dripping from around the doorsill.

He's been in there a long time, Zac told himself grimly. Something might have happened. Merlin is not a man of steel, or a man of bronze, hardly even a man of aluminum foil. He could be hurt. He might have made a mistake. Those are desperate men in there.

Zac squared his shoulders.

"It's up to me," he said.

He took a deep breath. "And now I'll . . ."

I'll *what*? he asked himself.

Chapter Five

Zac turned the corner to the street Max Merlin lived on and pulled up in front of the house. As he turned off the switch, he smiled. Now I know why there's always a place or two in front of Merlin's house, he told himself. In a city where parking places are so precious that they are all but sold at auction, Zac had always thought it seemed odd there was always a spot right in front of the Victorian house. A little convenient magic on Merlin's part, Zac concluded.

As Zac hopped out he heard a honking and looked back to see his best friend Leo pulling up on his moped. "Hey, Zac!" Leo called out with a smile. "I was just—"

"Don't have time," Zac said, waving at him as he trotted up the steps.

"Hey, *Zac!* How did your date with Julie go? Hey?"

But Zac was opening the door. He hid the lock from Leo with his body and took out his own housekey as a pretense. The lock was actually opened by a short, little spell. In fact, it could *only* be opened by the short, little spell. Max Merlin had no burglar alarm. At least, not a conventional one.

"Zac!"

Zac heard his friend running up the steps and shut the door in his face. As he crossed the living room, he heard Leo pounding on the door and heard the *bing-bong* of the doorbell. But he paid no attention. Leo couldn't help and Zac couldn't let his friend know about the magic part.

Or who Max Merlin really was.

Or that he, Zachary Rogers, was a sorcerer's apprentice.

"Oh, he'd get a laugh out of *that*," Zac muttered as he opened the door to the Crystal Room.

"Where are they?" the boy said as he rummaged through the big, white, secret room. "You don't need them," he said, talking to the absent Merlin, "but I do!"

When you are just starting to do something, everything seems difficult, he thought. Merlin made it look so easy. Not a single hand wave, no chants, no explosive puffs of smoke—unless, of course, he wanted a theatrical effect—no rustling parchments.

"But he's had sixteen hundred years to get it together!" Zac mumbled resentfully. Every expert makes it look easy, Zac thought. Mohammed Ali, dancing around a ring. One of those Russian ballerinas. Willie Shoemaker, riding a winner. Manolete, the bullfighter. Arnold Palmer, Sugar Ray, Picasso . . .

They learned all the rules, understanding why the rules were The Rules. The Rules were rules because they usually worked. Then they took off from there.

Sometimes Zac thought he'd never make it as an apprentice. Even an apprentice to a garbage collector. There just isn't enough time, he sighed to himself. First, a guy has regular school and all the schoolwork they load on you. Then the job at the garage, doing lubes and oil changes, tune-ups and radiator cleaning. Then a guy had to have *some* kind of social life. Hang out with the guys, go out on a date once in a while. See the latest movies, listen to records.

"I mean, you gotta stay with it," Zac said, looking under a brassbound book. Already he was losing track of which singer was with what group. He shifted a pile of rolled-up Latin parchments and a cloud of dust billowed up, choking him.

"Ah . . . ah . . . ah-*choo*!"

A salamander in a nearby jar of alcohol curled the other way. A handmade pot shifted itself slightly, turning its lead seal.

"Aha!" Zac said, grabbing up a small book bound in a strange reptilian leather. It was the one he'd begun his magic education with.

And after all the regular stuff, he expects me to bone up for hours on, Zac grumbled to himself. The Objective Theory of Ethics, The Odic Force, The Planes of Illusion, Psychokinesis (Theory of and Application of), Metagnomes, Transposition of the Senses, Exteriorization of Motricity, The Physical Properties of Frogs . . .

"You don't see *him* checking up on stars or discarnate whoevers," Zac muttered, looking into a drawer. "No, he just *does* it like, like . . ." Then he chuckled. "Like *magic*!"

As he rummaged through the drawer he grinned. "Yeah, like magic." He waved a hand in the air. "Abracadabra! Sizz-boom-bah! *Whammo*!"

He took out a box and peered at the hand-written label. "Do not open until 1812," he read aloud. Tossing it back he said, "Must have forgotten about it." He pulled out a manuscript crossed seven times with red ribbons and sealed with black wax at every crossing. "*The Theory and Practice of Vulture Summoning*," he read. "Ech!"

Zac slammed the drawer shut. "It must be here somewhere. I saw it last week." He went over to the shelves and peered behind some of the volumes. Idly, he read some of the titles. *Grue. Travels in the Yomi, the Spirit World of Japan. Mushrooms and Toadstools of the World. Ideomorphs Made Easy. The True Adventures of Sir Galahad and the Search for the Holy Grail. The Discoverie of Witchcraft.*

He turned away in annoyance and his eye lit on a small drawstring bag of leather, lying half under a block of stone from the Great Pyramid of Giza, shaped as a small pyramid. Zac snatched it up and checked the contents. "Good" he muttered out loud with relief. He'd practiced with the substance before.

Then, with the bag and the book, he quickly left the Crystal Room. Back in Merlin's living quarters, he carefully closed the door and turned to go.

Bing-bong!

"Oh, no!"

"I see you, Zac! What's going on? Can I come in?"

Zac threw open the door. "Leo!"

"Something's up, I know it!" Leo leaned close, smiling. "You can tell me."

Zac brushed by him, slamming the door behind him. "Forget it, Leo. This is . . . uh, this is business. Mister Merlin wanted me to get, uh, this stuff . . ."

He ran down the steps and around to the driver's side of his borrowed jalopy, jumping in as he shouted, "Talk to you later!"

Zac pulled away as Leo came running down. The young man stood on the sidewalk, looking bewildered and feeling hurt. He watched his best friend drive away.

"Oh, yeah?" he said and trotted over to his moped. Cranking it up, he started following Zac.

What is happening in there? Zac said to himself as his car squealed around a corner. How much time do I have? Why hasn't Merlin zapped those guys? Is Julie all right?

He looked up at the bridge. The traffic was still pretty heavy, even at this time of night. People were getting out of theaters and going back across the bay to the bedroom communities of Piedmont, Lafayette, Orinda, and Kensington. Berkeley students were going home. Navy personnel were going back to the Oakland terminal. Lots of traffic.

Zac found a parking spot a hundred feet down from the cable anchorage and pulled in quickly. He was so preoccupied that he didn't hear the moped buzzing up the street after him, or its sudden stop.

Zac got out and walked toward the door, the book in one hand and the bag in the other. "First, the chant, then the sprinkling. Or is it the sprinkling, then the chant?" he asked himself.

Oh, Merlin made it look so easy! No props, no telltale giveaways. Things just happened. One thing Zac had learned was that magic, real magic, often was indistinguishable from accident, chance, coincidence.

The wind just happened to dislodge a pebble, which rolled out in the street and just happened to get flipped up by the wheel of a passing car. The pebble accidently went sailing through the window of this house, knocking over a glass of water on the dining table. This water ran onto the floor and coincidentally right on a worn spot on the lamp cord, shorting out the electricity, which made the house owner go to the store to get some new fuses, where he ran into a fuse-buying young woman who became his wife six weeks later.

No, Merlin just seemed to will it. Like Chris Evert Lloyd seemed to will the ball into the right part of the court. Or Joe Namath willing a football into the mobile hands of a receiver. Or Norman Rockwell willing Americana onto a canvas. It looked so easy, like Gene Kelly dancing.

He stood before the door. It was dark there, but he knew at least one small trick. Zac opened the book and said the phrase. The script written across the parchment pages seemed to glow dimly. Enough for him to see.

Let's see . . .

Revealing Hidden Treasure.
Opening Enchanted Casks.
Opening Time-lock Enchanted Casks.

Opening Brazen Doors. Zac stared at that a moment, then remembered that brazen meant bronze. He looked again at the door before him. Looked like steel.

Opening Doors Sealed by Wizards of the Second Rank.

Opening Doors Sealed by Wizards of the First Rank.

Nothing about opening ordinary doors. He flipped through the book, oblivious of a shadow moving up cautiously, car by car.

Nemedian Bedazzlements, he read. *Vanaheim Encirclements. Zingara and Koth Bemusements.* Zac flipped several more pages impatiently. No telling what was going on inside the anchorage.

Stygian Befoulments of the Circle of Wells. Poictesmedian Thralls. Removal of Wens. How to Beguile a Lion. True Pellucidarian Cures for the Common Beheading.

Zac made a growling noise and flipped still more pages. This, after all, was his primer. *Removing Ants and Snails from Your Property. Atvatabar Dream Seeds. How to Charm Birds. Overcoming Fortresses Held by the Enemy.* "Aha!"

Maybe not a fortress, but close!

The shadow moved silently from darkness

to darkness, then stopped a few feet away. "To overcome any fortress occupied by an enemy, you must first . . ." Zac's voice trailed off as his lips continued to move. "Uh-huh," he agreed once; then, "Right, logical." A bit later he mumbled, "Hmmm, didn't know it worked like that . . ."

Finally, he sighed and closed the book. He repeated the spell to himself and was about to scatter the powder from the sack before the door when a voice said quietly from the shadows, "Zac, what in blue blazes are you *doing*?"

"*Leo!*" Zac clutched at his chest. "You almost gave me a heart attack!"

Leo stood up, shaking his head. "I followed you."

"I can see that," Zac said, casually holding the book and the sack behind his back.

"What are you doing here? Reading out of some old book, standing out here under the bridge like some sort of troll . . ." He shook his head. "Bananas. Zonkers. Over the hill. Round the bend." He stepped up close and peered at his friend's shadowed face. "You have not been acting normal lately, y'know. Spaced, actually . . . uh, you haven't been—?"

Zac shook his head vigorously. "What? Me?

No, are you kidding? Never! No, I'm, uh, well, I'm studying for the school play. That's it, right."

"Oh? What's the play?" Leo reached for the book, but Zac turned away. "No, it's a secret, I mean, uh, it's a surprise."

"Pretty nifty, though. Looked like a book with its own reading light."

"Yeah, well, it's new. I mean, a pilot model. I, uh, I mean, listen, Leo—"

"Zachary Rogers, you are up to no good." Leo said it in a high, nasal voice, a fairly exact impression of Mr. Bannister, the principal of their former grammar school.

In spite of himself, Zac let a small laugh escape. The two boys *had* given Bannister a bad time. "Look, Leo, I can't let you get into this. I—"

"Into what?" Leo asked eagerly. "What's happening? What's going on?" He looked around with an expectant smile.

"Leo, I . . . uh, we . . . well, look, Leo, you gotta keep this a secret, okay?"

"Cross my heart and hope to be on the cover of *People* magazine."

"Okay," Zac said, eyeing his friend suspiciously. "Well, Julie and I—"

"Julie and me."

"*We* were walking around here and—"

"On a date? Here?" Leo looked around incredulously. "This is not the most romantic spot in the city, Zac."

"I just wanted to . . . oh, never mind. We were here and there were some guys. Thugs. Crooks. They grabbed Julie and—"

"And what?" Leo said, aghast.

"Kidnapped her. In there." Zac pointed at the monolithic cement structure. "They're going to blow up the bridge if they don't get some kind of ransom. I gotta get in and rescue her and, uh, and Mister Merlin."

"*Max* is here?" He looked sideways at Zac. "I know her family is kinda strict, but I never thought they'd send an adult along!"

"They didn't. Mister Merlin got into this voluntarily . . ."

"And you let him? On a date with Julie?"

"Leo, listen to me. It isn't like that. These bad guys have Julie and Mister Merlin inside. If we don't rescue them they'll be killed!"

"I'll go for the cops!"

"No!" Zac said, grabbing Leo's arm. "Listen, no cops. They told me Julie would get killed for sure." He pulled Leo close. "Look, there might be more of them. You go down the street a-ways and if you see anything suspicious, whistle."

"What kind of whistle? I can't do any birdcalls or anything. I can bark like a dog. Sorta."

"Fine, bark like a dog. I'm going to see if I can get them out of there. As soon as the police find out what's going on, they are going to flock here like homing pigeons. Then Julie will be caught in between!"

"Well, how are they going to get away? They must have some tricky plan, huh? You gonna find that out?"

"I don't know, Leo—just go down there and watch."

"Right!" He gave Zac a military salute and started running, then turned and ran back. "Dog or bird?"

"Huh? Oh, uh, dog. Definitely dog."

"Any particular breed?"

"*Leo*—go!"

"Aye-aye."

Zac watched his friend trot down the street, then squat in the shadows. Carefully, Zac brought out the book. As he went toward the door he decided he better do more checking. He pressed his ear to the cold steel door.

Inside, Merlin was trying to get his

thoughts together. It was amazingly hard. It seemed as though a winged dragon was using the inside of his skull as a racetrack and several bees were practicing barrel rolls in his ears.

"One more time," the old man said.

It started to rain again.

Red rain.

Julie screamed. Bozo said, "Blood! Blood? *Blood!*"

No one bothered to realize it was thin, like ink, not thick like blood.

"Shut those sprinklers off!" bellowed Gino.

"Boss, I don't know where the shutoff is!" Lefty yelled back.

"You shut it off last time!"

"No, I didn't—it just stopped!"

"What's up there?" said Charlie, almost knee deep in blood-red water.

Julie was quivering with fright. "Zac," she said aloud, "just come rescue me and let's go get dry and warm."

"It's getting deeper," Bozo said, looking down at his soaked clothing.

Outside, Zac Rogers had finished scattering the dust in a semicircle. "Why couldn't Max have done this?" he grumbled. "He wouldn't need all this rigamarole."

The semicircle complete, Zac prepared to start the spell.

Inside, Gino said, "Open the door! Let some of this stuff outta here before we all drown!"

"What did you say?" Bozo yelled back through the thunderous waterfall.

"Open . . . the . . . door!"

"Open the floor?"

"Door, door, you idiot!" Gino shouted, pointing.

"Oh, right." Bozo splashed over and unlocked the door and started to pull it open.

The water, as red as wine, poured out, flooding acrooss Zac's line of dust and knocking the young apprentice on his backside.

Chapter Six

Zac rolled over and got out of the main flood of water gushing through the door, going to the uphill side. "Now's my chance," he said and ducked through the doorway.

The water, rushing out, had tumbled all the people standing on the wet floor. The red rain, still cascading down, filled their eyes every time they looked up. Half blinded, Zac slipped along the wall toward the left-hand stairs to the low balcony.

The rain stopped. The old bum wired to the railing swayed. Julie bent toward him. "Are you all right?"

"Um? Curious, curious. I don't think that should happen at all."

"Close that door, Bozo!"

"Right, boss—just as soon as I can stand up."

"What should happen?" Julie asked, looking around. That was when she saw Zac, crouched low, edging past a soaking wet Charlie rubbing at his eyes. The sudden cessation of rain had exposed him.

"Urk!" Julie said, stifling an outcry. My goodness! He *was* coming to rescue her!

Zac slid over the top steps and landed flat on his face on the balcony, out of sight of the crooks. He looked at Max Merlin, wondering how the old man could have gotten into this predicament. Zac noticed the strong wire binding the magician.

Need snippers. Have no snippers. Need time. Have no time. I'd be full of holes before I unraveled six inches of the wire. I am in trouble, Zac told himself.

"Go up there and check her out, Charlie," Gino said.

"Right."

Zac looked around and saw nothing but glistening wet concrete. And the opening to the cable anchorage side rooms. Without thinking further, he squirmed inside, twisting around just in time to see a man walk up, still knuckling one eye, blinding him to Zac's presence.

Zac stood up cautiously and looked out. Three cursing men were trying to wring out their clothes. Gino was blaming everyone. Zac pulled back and looked around.

From the east, the foot-thick cable came into this long, narrow room. A few feet through the thick concrete wall it started to unravel, spraying out in twists of three, then those three unwound into more twists of three. The ends of these many cables were now buried in the opposite wall. The floor slanted up to meet the wall. The cables were painted red orange, like the Golden Gate, not silvery, like the Bay Bridge they were supporting. Three electric eyes bridged the open doorway, but Zac had slid in under them.

Then he saw them.

On more than a dozen of the cables going into the last wall, into the mountain of rock and concrete beyond, there were irregular lumps of what looked like modeling clay.

Plastic explosive!

Zac had seen a lot of movies; he knew what it looked like. A wire linked each glob to a black box. A wire trailed out of the doorway from the box. Zac could simply yank the wire loose and disable at least one of the charges. If he could get across to the other side . . .

"Lefty—go check the charges. See if that water ruined everything."

"Aw, Gino, I had everything sealed. Nothing can hurt that plastic."

"Go check," Gino said in a deadly voice.

"Right," Lefty responded.

Zac heard footsteps trotting up the stairs and shrank back. There was no place to hide and no time!

Then the steps faded into the opposite cable room, the twin of the one he was in, but the one toward downtown. Zac had a reprieve, but only for a few seconds. He looked around frantically.

Lefty walked quickly across the balcony, looking down a few feet into the general area. Only an inch or two of water remained. The door sill was too high to let it out and Bozo closed it with a loud slam.

"And lock it!" Gino snapped.

"Right, boss."

"Please," Julie said. "Uh, mister? Lefty?"

"Sir Lyonel," Merlin said, squinting and swaying slightly.

"Uh, yeah?"

"Couldn't we—"

"*Lefty!* Stop fooling around. Go check!"

"Right, boss." He turned and marched into the other side room and Julie's face fell. She hadn't even had a chance to try out her feminine wiles, or anything else.

A few moments later, Lefty came out and announced to Gino, "Hey, like I said, everything's fine. Dry. Ready to go. One push on the button box, Gino, and the charges will blow two dozen of them cables. The weight of the bridge will pull the rest out like you tripped over a lamp cord. *Blue-eeee!*"

Lefty trotted down, laughing. "What a score! My rep will be made! The man who blew the Bay Bridge!"

Julie looked toward the side room. Where had Zac hidden?

In the small, narrow room, Zac swung down from the end where the full cable came in. Up there, despite the shadows, he was in clear view but none of the criminals happened to look in his direction.

Cautiously, Zac looked at the door and saw Julie staring at him. He put his finger to his lips and shook his head, then slipped back into the shadows again. He pulled out his leatherbound book and stared at it.

Okay, hot shot, now what?

You aren't good enough to step out there and paralyze all four of those crooks in one zap. You aren't even sure enough not to get stage fright and end up giving them a plague of warts.

What to do, what to do?

"Fair maiden, and thou art indeed fair—" Merlin began.

Julie stared at him in surprise. If this was some kind of disguise, it was a humdinger, whatever a humdinger was.

"I will summon a dragon to bear you off to a safer clime," Merlin said, gesturing gallantly toward her. Only he swayed and almost fell.

Near San Francisco International Airport a PSA jetliner coming in on the scheduled flight path had trouble with a flock of birds . . . inside the plane.

In Daly City, near the Pacific, every other house in the westernmost block turned green. Including the cars in the driveways and six poodles.

In the Mission District, fourteen winos, warming themselves by a fire, suddenly heard a roar that was too loud to be merely coming from the flames.

And something large struck the cable anchorage exterior. Down the street, Leo was twisting the red water out of his shirt, having been caught by accident. He heard the noise, which was something like a sack of pineapples the size of a Cadillac hitting a wall. All he saw was some shadows, and something like a big bird. But everything was gone and all was quiet again in moments.

"Oops," said Merlin.

Julie squatted down and got as close to the old garage mechanic as she could. "Uh, Mister Merlin—are you, ah, drunk?"

"Drunk?" Merlin shouted, making Gino look around with a scowl. "You think me drunk, wench? I'll have you know I have put that notorious drunkard Voltaire under the table. I was criticizing his *Candide* and we—"

"Hey! Old man! Cool it," Gino said.

Merlin looked around in bewilderment. "Where am I?"

"People really do say that, I guess," Julie said in wonderment. She looked toward where Zac was hidden. At any moment he would come bursting out, guns blazing, and—

Zac Rogers never fired a gun in his life, she thought. He'll be killed.

He'll burst out with his sword waving and—

No swords, either. Knowing Zac, she thought, he'll fall over it and hurt himself.

Then he'll . . .

He'll . . .

Well, he'll do something . . .

Zac was trying. The trouble was, he couldn't think of anything. Somehow he thought the rescue would be easier. It always was for heroes. In the movies, anyway. Dumb guards. Stolen weapons.

Then he heard Gino talking as he marched up the steps. Frantically, Zac climbed up the cables, as rigid as steel rods with the pressure. He hid again on the thick cable, stretching out to conceal himself better.

Gino came into the side room, pulling Lefty with him. He spoke low.

"Look, Lefty, I don't want the straights to hear. It always keeps 'em easier to handle if they think everything's cool."

Lefty nodded nervously, not knowing what was coming next.

"Now listen up, Lefty," Gino hurried on. "Look, we gotta hold her—the bum's a zero—until the ransom is paid and we make our getaway. Then we'll hafta frost her. She knows our faces."

Lefty nodded reluctantly. "Yeah, but she's just a kid, Gino."

"Old enough for eyes, old enough to finger you in a courtroom, man."

"Yeah, yeah. But, gee."

"Bargaining power, man. They will shoot a little less quickly if a civilian is in the middle. You wanna get shot, man? No, you don't wanna get shot." He pulled at Lefty's shirt. "Look, this is really you and me, right? Me the brains, you the fingers. Bozo, Pinky, Charlie, they're spearcarriers, dig? Protection. *We* hang onto the chick, just in case."

"The old bum?"

"He's harmless, even if he does mumble a lot. They might think he's some prominent citizen and we can use him as a shield. If worst comes to worst."

"They're gonna be all over us there, soon as Pinky drops off the tape."

"Stick to the plan. That's what we do—stick to the plan. We'll get outta here, live like kings, right?"

"Right," Lefty said without feeling.

Gino slapped Lefty on the shoulder and they left without noticing the frightened youth lying on the cable.

They're going to kill Julie!

And Merlin!

But Mister Merlin can take care of himself and Julie is just a kid.

Zac shook his head, letting himself down silently. They were not going to get away with it. I, Zachary Rogers, Apprentice Wizard, will take care of everything!

Zac crept over to the light from the main room and got out his directions book.

Darkening the Moon. Curing a King of Gout. Curing a Queen of Dyspepsia. Curing any Noble Person of Doubts About the Legitimacy of the Throne. Aha!

Rescuing Maidens Prepared for Sacrifice. He scanned the directions and his heart fell. The purification rites alone would take all night! Merlin—why did you let them bop you?

Rescuing Maidens, General Instructions. Zac blinked. All it said was, "Think twice."

Think twice? What did that mean? Don't

do it? Surely not! Maidens were for rescuing and that used to be one of their functions, as far as history and legend would have it.

But what about today? Women's liberation. The raising of consciousness by both genders. Equality. Maybe she'd prefer to rescue herself.

Zac peered out cautiously, staying well back. She was still wired up. Merlin was still blinking and muttering.

No, it's up to me, Zac argued with himself, and gulped.

They have guns.

You have the tradition of magic that goes back to the dimmest memory of man.

Yeah, but I don't know it too well.

Nevertheless, you are here. You are the only one.

And I volunteered, Zac told himself.

He reopened the book and squinted at it in the bad light. He was afraid to have the letters glow.

Rescuing Maidens, General Instructions. Part One. First, find a maiden not only suitable for rescuing but one you want to rescue. Two, make certain of her dire circumstances—do not blunder into a sticky and embarrassing situation. There *are* women who prefer zest in their lives and seek out the socially crude for companionship. Three, proceed as follows.

Frowning in the lackluster light reflected from the main room, Zac squinted out at the room again. He didn't notice a stiff parchment page flip over.

He looked down and started the spell.

Bozo's pants caught fire.

Charlie's shirt started trying to crawl over his head.

Bozo developed a seething hatred toward his feet and began stomping them.

Gino's gun began firing. In his pants.

Gino yanked the weapon out of his smoking trousers, yelling at the flashburns.

Ka-poom! Silenced or not, it was loud enough in the concrete room. *Ka-poom! Ka-poom! Whinnnninnng!*

Gino held it up, letting the automatic expend its last rounds up toward the dark recesses of the very high chamber. *Ka-pow!* Each shot was slightly louder than the previous one as the silencer's baffles compacted. Unlike in the movies, a real silencer only works well for a shot or two, then it starts getting noisy.

Ka-pinnng!

The gun fell silent. Gino stared at it as if it were a snake. "Double-crossing, no-good—" he muttered as he reached in his pocket for more ammunition.

"Gino!" Bozo yelled, rolling in the thin pool of red water, trying to extinguish his burning trousers. "Charlie!"

Charlie had fought free of the shirt, which now seemed to be swimming through the water, slowing down as it got wetter.

They all looked at Lefty, to whom nothing had happened. "What's going on, man?" Charlie said. "This is no time for tricks!"

"I didn't do nuthin," protested Lefty.

"You didn't do *anything*," corrected Merlin.

"See, the old bum seen it, too. I didn't do nuthin."

Merlin's eyes rolled upward. "What is knighthood coming to? They won't use forks and they can't keep their grammar straight."

Zac, back in the shadows, made a face. Blew that one, hotshot! Think you're Merlin, huh? Think you can take his place? Not likely, twerp! Not until you are *smooth!*

Zac scampered through his book again. *Philosophical Aspects of Invisibility, Extrac-*

ted *from the Rosarium Philophorum.* Nope. *Morgen Le Fey's Favorite Recipe for Frog Soup.* No. *Dreams and Enchantments Suitable for Beguiling Men of Less Than Noble Intelligence.* Might do. What else is there?

Zac noticed a hasty scrawl in the margins of the book, and it looked like Merlin's handwriting. "In the combat between wisdom and feeling, wisdom never wins."

Oh, dear, thought Zac. But he read on. *Antidotes Against Dark Magic. Antidotes Against Degenerate Teeth. Antidotes Against Frogs Who Hunt in Packs.*

Zac uttered a low growl of frustration. He flipped back to the section on *Beguiling Men* and began to scan quickly through the words, trying to learn it fast.

The trouble was, Zac didn't learn it perfectly.

When he tried it, Bozo fell asleep. Charlie trapped his shirt and wrestled with it until it went limp; then he squeezed out the water and put it on. Lefty took a step up the stairs and started floating off. Gino stared at Lefty, then had an irresistible urge to stand in the corner.

"Hey, hey!" Lefty said. "Hey, I'm floating! I'm floating!"

"What are you on?" Charlie asked suspiciously. "You got something you didn't share?"

"Ready or not, here I come," Gino said, turning around. His face fell. "You bums didn't hide!" His gun came out. "Now, listen. You hide or I'll blow your gizzards out!"

"Right, boss," Charlie said and his shirt climbed up over his face. Bozo was still asleep and Lefty had his eyes closed. When Gino counted to ten and turned around he didn't see Lefty at all. "Hey, great! Got you, Bozo, but where's Charlie and Lefty?" He was standing three feet from the shirt-covered Charlie, who didn't say a thing.

Gino was about to go search the side rooms when he heard a whimper. He looked up and saw the bottoms of Lefty's shoes. "Lefty! Gotcha! Come on down!"

"Boss . . . uh . . . boss?"

"Yeah, yeah? Where's Charlie?"

"Boss . . . I . . . I can't come down."

"C'mon, Lefty, stop fooling around, I see you up there. Come help me look for Charlie."

"Boss, I . . ."

"Never mind, I'll find him."

Before Zac could move, Gino had bounded up the steps and into the side room. And looked right at Zachary Rogers, Apprentice Wizard. "Hey! Who are you?" The gun came out like a snake. "Hey, you're the punk outside!" He rammed the silencer up to Zac's nose. "How'd you get in here?"

"I . . . I . . . I . . . uh . . ."

"Get in there!" Gino snarled, grabbing Zac and throwing him through the doorway. Then he let out a bellow. "Who opened the door? And where's the old bum?"

Chapter Seven

Julie, still wired to the railing, was staring up at the soles of Lefty's feet. "How did he do that?" she asked no one in particular.

"Hey, Charlie! Where are you?"

"Right here, boss!"

"Where?"

"Here." Charlie pulled down his shirt and grinned at Gino. "Did I win?"

"How'd the old guy get out?" Gino flicked his hand at the wires that had bound Merlin to the railing. They weren't even unraveled. "Close that door!"

"Right, boss!" Bozo said, jumping up and colliding into Charlie, bent on the same mission. The door, despite their efforts, was slammed shut and relocked.

Gino snarled at Zac, who was wide-eyed, his eyes staring at the gun barrel. "Okay, punk, what's going on here?"

"What's going on here is obvious," Julie said haughtily, recovering from her boggling at Lefty, and—in fact—putting it safely out of her mind. There are some things you are better off not understanding. Like how the meat gets in the sausage skin. Or how Jerry Lewis keeps making movies.

"Oh, yeah?" Gino growled.

"You are vicious thugs and this is the man come to rescue me."

"*Man?*" laughed Gino. "Man? Oh, come on, sister!"

"You are miscreants of the first water and you shall be punished for this!"

Gino leered. "The *right* line, chickie, is, 'You'll never get away with this.'"

"You'll never get away with this! Thank you."

"You're welcome. Charlie, wire the new kid to the railing. He's better than the bum."

"What about the bum, boss?" Bozo asked. "Should I go finish him off?"

Gino looked at his watch. "Never mind. No one will pick him up, and it's a long walk to any cop from here. Any minute now Pinky'll be back." He leered. "Then the fun starts."

Max Merlin sat on the curb and stared at the cable anchorage across the street. What did all this mean? Where was Zac? Didn't they come here for some reason? Oh, yes, right. Rescuing a maiden, of course. Julie, wasn't it?

These young lads. Just couldn't keep them home. One rumor of a maiden who needed rescuing and off they went—knight, squire, apprentice, the works. Ego-trips, the lot of them. Lusty derring-do for the hand of maiden fair.

If they only knew! You didn't have to fight. a dragon to win fair maiden. Just look and act as if you could. And would. They don't really want you to go fight, but they love the idea that you would.

Over them, of course.

Merlin heard footsteps and looked up to see Leo, wearing wet and wrinkled clothes. "Mister Merlin? Is that you?"

"Hello, Leo," Merlin said wearily. This one was Zac's friend, wasn't he? Pest. Nosy. Liked puns. And puns were nature's way of making you appreciate real humor. Liked onions on his fast-food hamburger, too, he noted.

"Mister Merlin, what's going on tonight?"

"You don't know?"

"No."

"Oh, I thought you'd tell me. I'm kind of fuzzy right now. Kind of blurry. What, uh, what do you think happened?"

"Well . . ." Leo took a deep breath and tried to get it all straight. "Zac and Julie were here and Julie got snatched by some bad guys who are going to blow up the bridge if they don't get some big ransom and Zac is afraid for Julie and he went in and all this red water came out and now here you are."

"Oh," said Merlin. "Is that all?"

"All? All?" Leo Samuels was astonished. "Isn't that enough?"

"Uh-huh," Merlin said abstractly. "Hm. Yes. It's beginning to come back." He looked at Leo. "Yes, I remember you now. Ride a moped. Noisy thing. Zooming around."

"Yes, sir," Leo mumbled. "But Zac and Julie . . ."

"No cops."

"Uh, that's what Zac said. I don't see why—"

"There's a reason." The old man got slowly to his feet, holding onto the bumper of a car.

"Listen, Mister Merlin, I don't mean to be,

uh, critical, but you look like ... well, you look like a bum. And that," he said, indicating Merlin's unshaved jaw and the scraggly mustache. "You looked pretty good yesterday."

Merlin rubbed his face, his eyes widening. "Oh ... uh, yes. Must be the light here. Tricky. Now look, Leon—"

"Leo. Leo Samuels?"

"Leo, yes." He closed his eyes and swayed a bit. Leo grabbed his arm.

"Are you okay, Mister Merlin? Do you need a doctor? Maybe I should call an ambulance or something?"

"No, no," Merlin said quickly. "Just as soon as I get my wits about me, I'll ... listen, Len—"

"Leo. L-E-O. Means lion. Leon does, too. Leonard means 'bold lion.'"

"My name is Merlin," the magician said, his eyes half-lidded.

"Yes, sir, I know, but—"

"Long time ago they said Marwin, Mervin, Marlin." The old man lifted his head and his voice got stronger as he declaimed, "'She call'd him lord and liege/Her seer, her bard, her silver star of eve/Her god, her Merlin.'" He sighed and his shoulders slumped. In a flat voice he said, "*Idylls of the King:* Vivien, by Alfred, Lord Tennyson."

Leo looked around nervously. "Mister Merlin, I think we better—"

"Never really knew him, y'know, Tennyson. I was in France then. Think I met him once, though, at some party. Good-looking chap, too good-looking for his own good. Knew Shelley, though, of course. Knew his second wife better. Always thought it odd. Man's wife writes a horror story, gets better known for that than anything the lad did his whole life. Ironic."

"Sir, I—"

"*Frankenstein*, boy, *Frankenstein*. Mary Wollstonecraft Shelley. She wrote *Frankenstein*, y'know. Clever idea, really. Quite different in her day."

"Mister Mer—"

"Don't interrupt, boy. You'll never learn anything by interrupting. Now, I—"

"*Mister Merlin*," Leo said desperately. "Zac's in there, and Julie, and those bad guys—"

"Of course, I know, I know. You think I'm a doddering old man?" Merlin straightened his shoulders. "Arthur thought I was mad, too, but he couldn't get along without me.

Look what happened when I wasn't around."

"Arthur who? Art Garfunkel? Art Mooney? Bea Arthur? Mister Merlin, please! This is serious!"

"Life is serious, lad. Except for the parts that are funny. Did I ever tell you the one about Sir Kay the Seneschal and the milk-maid? It seems that Sir Kay loved blood pudding and—"

"Mister Merlinnnn!" Leo grabbed his arm and the old man turned his head slowly to look at him.

"Oh. Oh, yes. Leon. Bold lion. Good name. *Coeur de Lion,* 'the lion-hearted.' That was Richard's name, y'know, lad. Stout fellow but a bit crude. But then it was, in those days . . ."

"Mister Merlin, this is no time for rapping about the old days. We gotta do something!" He shook Merlin's arm. "Tell me what to do!"

Merlin looked at him a long time without expression. Then he nodded, slowly. "You are exactly right. A time for action." He looked around at the cable anchorage. "Hm. Yes. Getting it now. Look, lad, there's . . . something I need."

"What? I'll get it! Guns? Gas? Flak jackets? What?"

"No, no. I need . . ." He seemed to pause for a moment and a crafty expression came over his face. "I need sausages."

"*Sausages?*" Leo was astounded. "Is . . . is that a term for something? Like 'pineapple' for hand grenade?"

"No, sausages. Like you eat. Polish sausages, any kind."

"Now? This time of night?"

"There are markets open. This is a great metropolitan city."

"Well, okay, but how many?"

"Lots."

"How many is 'lots'? Pounds, feet, numbers, what?"

"Um . . ." Merlin eyed the entrance to the cable anchorage, "As many as it takes to go all the way around the doorway there."

Leo looked it over. "Ten, twenty . . . double across the . . . another ten. About thirty feet."

"Make it forty. No, forty-five," Merlin said.

"Forty-five feet of sausages," Leo said, as if he couldn't believe it.

"Fifty to be certain," Merlin added.

Leo dug into his pocket. "Uh, I got . . . ten, twenty-five . . . I have three dollars and twenty-five cents. I don't think that's enough."

"Not to worry," Merlin said, reaching into his pocket and pulling out a coin, dropping it into Leo's palm.

The youth stared at it. "That's a gold coin. I can't spend that in the supermarket. Not at this hour, that's for sure."

"Oh," Merlin said, focusing his eyes. He frowned a bit, then dug into another pocket and pulled out a fistful of silver dollars. Again, Leo stared.

"Eighteen-eighty-eight silver dollars," he said reverently. "These are worth a fortune! They're mint, too! Mister Merlin, I—"

"Go, lad. Go at once! I must have the sausages."

"You have a plan?" Leo was spilling the heavy coins into his pockets.

"I have a plan," Merlin said with dignity and confidence. Leo nodded briskly and trotted to his moped and was off in a blurt of noise.

Then Merlin sat down. What was his plan?

He stared at the entrance. It seemed to go in and out of focus. His head hurt terribly. He couldn't seem to concentrate. But he knew Zac was inside, and the Lady Julie. And there was something about villains ...

As soon as Merlin more or less forgot about him, Lefty came falling from the shadows. Luckily for him, but unluckily for Bozo, who was standing under him, telling him to cut it out, he landed with Bozo as the cushion.

"What were you doing up there?" Gino demanded. "Climbing around, playing again, huh?" Lefty looked shamefaced. He and Gino had been children together. Gino had always been the leader and Lefty had always done the dirty work. He had done all the tree-climbing to scout for the right kind of windows to peek in. He had done all the climbing through transoms and air ducts and over fences when they set out on their life of crime.

But despite the advantages of having a catlike ability to climb, Lefty had never felt superior to Gino, who always fell off or out or in. As a result, Gino tended to belittle any climbing Lefty did.

"Well, what were you doing?" Gino demanded.

Lefty knew it was going to be hard to explain. No one would believe him, anyway. He hadn't climbed at all. Rather, his trousers had lifted up and he had stayed in them. It was a very odd sensation.

"Uh, nothing," he said. "Just fooling around."

Well, knock it off and keep your eyes open, knothead."

Zac wanted badly to tell Julie not to worry. At this very moment the greatest magician in the world was gathering the mighty forces at his command. All hell would break loose at any moment. The walls would sunder, the Bad Guys would be encased in steel bands, and the floor would swallow them.

But nothing was happening.

The wire cut into his wrists. His textbook on magic was lying in a damp spot on the balcony, kicked aside and ignored. There wasn't a single spell that came to mind.

I wish I had paid more attention, Zac said to himself. From now on I will. I'll learn every spell by heart. I'll practice it until I can do it like Mister Merlin, he told himself. Effortless and swift, just like a stage magician.

Zac sniffed. Stage magicians! Hah! Little they know! Tricksters! Sleight-of-hand bafflements! They shouldn't be allowed to use the term "magician." Then Zac remembered Merlin had told him that there *was* one stage magician who was, indeed, a real magician, which explained his popularity.

But that wasn't helping him to get Julie out of this pickle. He turned to Julie and said in a low whisper, "Keep an eye on them."

She looked down where Gino was pacing around and the others were sitting dejected on the steps, still wet. Bozo was extracting the contents of his pockets and trying to dry them out. She nodded to Zac. "I'll stand guard. You work on the wires."

But Zac had no intention of being so obvious. They were, after all, standing in plain sight. He turned his back to Julie, at least as much as he could, with his wrists wired to the railing. He stared at the magic textbook lying there.

And it moved.

He jumped, more than a little surprised that his telekinetic effort actually worked.

Only an inch, but hey!

He concentrated again and the book skidded three inches, then three more, then almost hopped six. Zac was delighted! He looked around. Julie was watching the thugs in casual sweeps of her pretty head.

Zac looked at the book and it slid over in a rush and thumped into his foot. He suppressed an exclamation and then stared at the book some more. The cover flipped open and the pages began turning.

Shannarian Blights. How and Why to Irritate a Dragon. The Major Mysteries of the Empire of the Frogs. On Obtaining Entrance to Sporting Events. Magical Swords, a Checklist.

Zac uttered a small growl of frustration, then looked quickly around. Julie gave him a glance, then looked down to see what he was doing about the wires. "What are you doing?" she said through clenched teeth and smiling lips. "Get on with it!"

The pages blew by, as if a wind were turning them. *Theogony in Modern Times. Queen Guinevere's Beauty Secrets for a More Beauteous Skin. Lemurian Curses. The Dis-*

corporation of Evil Bonds. The Twelve Ways to Gain the Affection of Maidens.

Zac stopped at that one. The frustrating thing about the book Merlin had given him on the first day of training was that sometimes there were pages missing. You'd go back to look something up and it wouldn't be there. No pages torn out, but between *Principles of Geometric Magic* and *Dressage for Winged Horses* there might be *Alchemic Formulae for the Transmutation of Elements* one time and *Phaldorian Dissertations on the Importance of Hair* the next time. You never knew.

Zac stared at the script outlining the Twelve Ways, but a hidden wind turned the page. When he willed the page to turn back, it was now a short, illustrated passage on *Symbolic Fertility*. Zac grumbled to himself and forced the pages back to *The Discorporation of Evil Bonds*.

Discorporation did mean "disintegration," didn't it?

Zac looked down at the page, his lips moving silently. Then he straightened, closed his eyes, and said the words in his mind, concentrating with great effort.

The wires around his wrists turned to

barbed wire and he yelped. They went back to electric wire, softer, but still quite immobilizing.

"Zac, what's wrong?" Julie said, still smiling down at the crooks.

"Nothing, nothing."

"Do something. That Pinky person will be here any minute and the cops soon after and after that we're just pawns. They'll be watching us more closely, or ... or we'll be shields!"

"Yeah, yeah ... lemme concentrate."

"On what? Get the wires off and—"

"Julie!" Zac pleaded in an intensely quiet voice.

Oh, if I could only just tell her and do it right out in the open, he thought. But Merlin had cautioned him about keeping everything secret.

"If any of these yahoos know—or even *suspect*—what or who I am, I'll never have a moment's peace. Now you know why all those comic-book superheroes have a secret identity—so they can have some peace at home. Go out to a movie or a nice restaurant without being asked questions, without being asked to save someone or do something. We don't need publicity."

Zac agreed, but right now it didn't seem like such a bad idea to have Julie know, to get it done quickly. He stared down again at the words on the page. It wasn't just the words, he knew, but the timing, the tempo or pace, the rhythm, the way you said the words, even if the saying was just in your mind.

He started again.

And there was a pounding on the door.

Chapter Eight

The thumping froze all the crooks with hands on their guns.

Thump. Thump. Thump. Pause. *Thump.* Pause. *Thump, thump.*

"It's Pinky. Let him in," ordered Gino.

Bozo unlocked the door and swung it cautiously open. A small, ratty-looking man stuck his head in. "All set," he announced. "The station got the tape. I made the call from the box across the street, then went up the street and saw the deejay come out and get it from where I taped it."

"Good job," Gino said. "How long ago was that?"

"Fifteen, eighteen minutes. It was hard getting through. He's one of those talk-show guys, y'know? Had on some author with a book on sex and astrology. That gets 'em all out. Finally got through. Well, see you guys. You know where to send my part."

"Hey, wait a minute," Bozo said, grabbing Pinky's collar. The pink-faced man looked up at him in surprise.

"You guys don't need me. I ain't no torpedo."

"You're in this with us," Bozo growled.

"Let him go," Gino ordered. "If anything goes wrong, we'll need someone out there to handle things. Right, Pinky?"

"Uh, right, Gino. Right." The small man looked nervous. "Good idea. But, hey, heh-heh-heh, nothing will go wrong. You guys got it all figured out. The police chief brings the ransom and you use him as a cover while you have the city set up a jet at the airport, only you're really going up the Sacramento River in a boat!" He tapped his forehead. "Thinking, Gino, thinking!"

"I let him go, boss?" Bozo asked reluctantly. Gino nodded and Bozo released the little man. Pinky saluted with one finger and ducked back out. Bozo closed the door.

Outside, Merlin watched the little man hop back into his Mazda and go humming off.

I should have acted, Merlin thought. Gone through the door like thunder. He shook his head. He was slowing up. His head hurt. But I've got to rescue Sir Zachary and Lady Julie. Modred has them prisoner.

The old magician stood up straight and concentrated on the door. It seemed to waver for a second, like an effect in a bad science fiction movie, then become solid again.

"Drat!" Merlin said aloud. He started concentrating again.

Go back to basics, he told himself. First principles. Elementals. Never mind the pain in the head. Never mind the sick feeling in the stomach. Concentrate . . .

In the downtown business district, a stockbroker, coming down the elevator in the Transamerica Building after a long day's work, felt the traveling box come to a halt. The doors hissed open and he stepped out into the lobby.

Only it wasn't the lobby. It was a torture chamber.

Dank stone walls with clusters of rings. From the rings hung chains and in the manacles at the ends of the chains were skeletons. Some of the skeletons were evidently more recent than others.

A pair of thickly muscled men, bare-chested and wearing black hoods and black tights, turned to look at him. Fire from a brazier reddened their sweaty skin. Stretched on the rack in front of them was that lovely brunette from Bergstresser and Randall. What they were doing wasn't nice. The place smelled terrible.

"Oh, pardon me," the stockbroker said and stepped back into the elevator. He punched *Lobby* again and it seemed like hours before the doors swished shut. The whole time the young woman was cursing at her torturers in pithy, fierce phrases.

He felt the elevator go up one floor. He waited with dread for the doors to open. But when they did, it was the same, pristine, antiseptic lobby he had always known. He walked out, signed out with the guard, and went out into the street.

"I've been working too much," he said aloud. "Going to take a week off."

Merlin's lips compressed in a straight line. He'd never had so much trouble before. But then, he'd never been knocked out before, either. "I don't know how those TV detectives do it, week after week," he said aloud.

Again, he tried.

At the corner of Castro and 18th Street, forty-one men and seven women felt an unpleasant prickling on certain areas of their bodies. There was a rush to various rest rooms, where forty-eight people found they now had three-color tattoos of twelve tiny swords in a circle around a crown.

On Atalaya Terrace a young cartoonist started drawing nothing but boffo gags about knights, elves, wizards, maidens in distress, and talking dragons.

"Elf snits!" cursed Merlin. "Dragon plop!"

He forced himself to calm down. Everything is going wrong, he thought. There is something awry. It must be my head. The spells are of the best quality, but they are ricocheting off into the night, causing all sorts of damage and trouble.

Actually, of course, the tattoos were to become the talk of the area, the cartoonist would win a Hugo, and the stockbroker would fall in love with the brunette woman, who would play hard to get, thus making his life more interesting.

But right then, in the darkened street, under the innocent hum of bridge traffic overhead, things seemed pretty grim.

Inside, by the balcony railing, Zac Rogers was trying to get things right.

First, the Lemurian spell-breaker, then the Atlantean verification, and finally, the discorporation, using the Asgardian Sword Spell.

"Right," Zac said.

"What?"

"Nothing, I . . . just keep watch."

"I am keeping watch," Julie muttered impatiently, but what are you doing?" She looked down, following his gaze, and saw the book at his feet. "Zac! I know you love reading, but this is ridiculous! Get us out of here!"

Really! she thought. And to think I thought he would rescue me! Zac Rogers couldn't rescue a whale in a cup of water! I'm just going to have to get us out of here. Wonder Woman could. Jane Fonda could, I bet. The Bionic Woman, certainly.

It did not occur to Julie that two of those women had superpowers and the other, a clever script. But none of them would have faulted her for at least trying to take things into her own hands.

If only her hands weren't wired together . . .

Meanwhile, Zac was trying hard. He practiced the spell carefully, then closed his eyes, better to concentrate, and began.

The wires around their wrists grew a little warm, which made Julie yelp. "Hey, quiet down," Gino growled. He had more important things on his mind than a couple of dingy kids. The cops would be showing up soon enough. There were only two anchorages to this bridge, this one and the one on the other end, on Yerba Buena Island.

Julie danced around a little, biting at her lip as the wires heated up. "Zac!" she whispered. "What are you doing?"

"I'm . . ." He couldn't tell her. Partially because it wasn't necessary that she know and partially because he didn't know. The wires *were* becoming rather uncomfortably hot.

Then they weren't there any more and Zac discovered at once that he had not thought out the next step.

There was no place to go.

Merlin pressed his fingertips to his head. "Two things they never figured out," he muttered, referring to the ancient magician-researchers. "How to cure the common cold and how to get rid of a headache."

He tried unsuccessfully to thrust aside the blurring effect of the pain in his skull, and to concentrate on freeing Zac and Julie. Teleporting them out was not feasible, first because Julie would surely suspect something and the other—for more pragmatic reasons—because the thickness of the concrete and steel building blunted and diffused his magic.

Immobilizing the miscreants inside was also not very effective, as he had discovered, and for the same reason. Merlin then remembered the first principle of understanding magic: Magic is the art of causing and controlling coincidence.

"For the want of a nail, the shoe was lost," he muttered. "The loss of the shoe led to the loss of the horse and thence to the loss of the kingdom in battle." He knew he was quoting incorrectly but he didn't care. It was the thought that counted.

Coincidence.

Merlin concentrated again, cutting through the blinding pain in his head . . .

. . . Gino's pacing carried droplets of water to one side of the center area, deepening the small pool left from the red rain. Bozo stepped into the pool and the liquid splashed up onto his socks. He sat down to squeeze his socks dry—again—and sat on the cartridge case empty from Gino's burst of gunfire. Yelling, he stood up suddenly and bumped into Charlie, who was knocked back against the wall, where he hit his head and was knocked out. . . .

Merlin smiled. It could be done, reinforced walls or not. He couldn't do the next thing that occurred to him—that of arranging the statistical possibility of all the air molecules in the room going to one side at once, leaving the crooks to flounder like fish out of water until they passed out. No telling where Zac and Julie were and he didn't want to hurt them.

So he tried the next thing that occurred to him. . .

Bending over Charlie, trying to shake

him awake, Bozo was bumped from behind by Lefty. Bozo was catapulted from his off-balance position and tried to stick his head through the wall. He fell atop the unconscious Charlie with a groan. . . .

Merlin grinned mischievously. This was more like it!

Two down, two to go!

But Merlin counted without the effects of his apprentice, one Zachary "The Klutz" Rogers.

Zac stared at the two suddenly unconscious crooks. "This is our chance," he said. "Run for the door!"

They sprinted to the end of the balcony and took the few steps in two jumps. Gino saw them out of the corner of his eye and whirled around, drawing his silenced automatic. Julie yiped and increased her speed. Zac braked to a halt and raised his hand to send a blast of fire in the direction of Gino.

Except that's not what happened.

First, Zac, in his haste, confused the Ninevah Firesword with the Secret of Charlemagne—the two spells were much alike, except for the atrocious grammar in the latter—and set the end of his forefinger afire.

Second, Merlin used an old trick of Sycorax, the witch-mother of Caliban, and tried to turn the clothing of the bad guys to iron, thus trapping them in immobile metal suits. But filtered through the steel and concrete, it turned all the metal in their clothing to cloth and their pants fell off.

Third, clutching at his sagging trousers, Gino's first shot was fired at the wall, high over the heads of the two fleeing youths.

Fourth, the bullet whinged and whacked its way around the chamber until it plopped down into the lap of the amazed Lefty. Who jumped up yelling, as the flattened slug was very hot.

Fifth, the same spell that had turned metal to cloth had softened and fused the door lock. Try as she could, Julie could not open the door.

Sixth, Lefty, hopping around, fell over, his legs entangled in his pants.

Seventh, he fell against Gino, just as Gino was moving in on Zac.

Eighth, the noise of the shot—now that the silencer was almost useless—was thunderous in the cement room, causing even Gino to flinch.

Ninth, the bullet's path, deflected from its

flight into the heart of Zachary Rogers, ricocheted off the wall and took a chunk out of the left-hand set of steps. No one thought much about the missing piece of step at the time. Too much was going on.

Tenth, Zac pulled at Julie and yanked her back toward the stairway as Gino, staggering under Lefty's weight, sought to shoot at them again.

Eleventh, Gino remembered he didn't wear shorts.

Twelfth, Zac and Julie made it into the protection of the side room.

Silence.

"What are you doing?" Gino said to Lefty.

"My pants fell down."

"I know your pants fell down. My pants fell down. The button and the zipper . . ." He looked down. They were metal again. Bent metal, but metal. He could have sworn they fell apart like cardboard. . . .

"Getcha pants on, this ain't no nudist camp," Gino snapped.

"At least I wear shorts," Lefty muttered.

"What?"

"I said, uh, that was a short, uh, time . . ."

"All right, you kids," Gino bellowed, waving his gun. "Come outta there, I seen you run in there!"

Huddled against the wall, Zac held Julie in his arms. It was a distracting experience, but he tried to focus on the immediate situation. If he had time, he supposed he could have used the old "We'll never get out of this alive" ploy and try some fool-around. But he didn't have time.

He heard Bozo and Charlie groan and start mumbling something. He heard Gino coming up the steps, saying. "Don't try nothin, you kids. I don't wanna hafta plug ya."

This is not a good situation, Zac told himself.

Merlin stood with hands on hips. "It didn't work. Maybe there is some sort of counterspell going." He cast his senses out, but perceived very little. No counterforces of any strength. None of the very distinctive vibrations of Morgen le Fey. There was a quiver from downtown where three hundred youths were having a new experience with something called The Force. Out in the Sunset District a reader of palms—totally unaware of her real powers as an adept—was telling a record promoter the next big thing in music would be computerized punk rock bands.

Nothing unusual. It had to be all his fault.

Merlin took a look down the street. It was taking forever to get fifty feet of sausage. He'd have to hurry.

He concentrated, focusing against the insistent pain.

Belshazzar, son of Nebuchadnezzar, Third Level Adept, lend me the power of your mind. . . .

Aphrodite, lend me your serenity. . . .

Chiron, your hooves . . .

The Seven Circle of the Chaldean Sorcerers, attend!

Merlin pointed at the steel door to the anchorage.

Thunder was heard over Sausalito.

Lightning in the Golden Gate.

Hailstones in Golden Gate Park.

Ripplings of reality along Union Street.

Chemical changes in smoky rooms.

Strange scratching noises in the bowels of BART.

Rustlings along Market Street.

Old books fell off shelves in the Mission District.

In an exhibition at the Legion of Honor, all the paint slid wetly off the contemporary paintings to the floor.

At the de Young Museum, two suits of armor tried to walk, and crashed to the polished floor.

At Fisherman's Wharf, in the Ripley's Believe It or Not Museum, nine people believed.

In the Ted E. Bear shop at Pier 39, all the bears growled.

And at the cable anchorage the clouds had boiled in, cloaking it all in impenetrable fog.

And the steel door went *pop*.

It opened slightly.

And Merlin heard the scream.

Chapter Nine

Merlin moved across the street, still wet from the red tide which had been released earlier. The scream did not come again, which somehow made it worse.

He touched the door with his fingertips. It swung silently open and he looked into the concrete chamber. Charlie and Bozo were on their feet, but staggering, with painful expressions on their faces as they held their hands to their throbbing heads. Lefty was busy buckling up his trousers. And Gino was holding a gun to Julie's head. No one seemed to be looking in Merlin's direction.

"Okay, punk, come out, easy now," Gino said. "I don't know how you got outta them wires, but next time we'll keep a closer watch on ya."

Zac came out, hands high. Gino had simply stuck the gun around the corner and said, "I start firing in five seconds."

Julie had uttered, "Yipe!" and hopped into the thug's clutches.

Zac was dejected. All their brilliant escape methods and no place to run. They might never get another chance. These are desperate, dangerous men, he thought. Never mind that they are also clumsy fools. A clumsy fool could be dangerous, too.

Well, Zac told himself, you are a clumsy fool—can you be dangerous?

Still no one looked at Merlin.

Which was not chance.

He didn't want to be looked at. Not yet. He had to find just the right moment. If only my head didn't hurt so much . . .

"You'll never get away with this!" Julie snapped.

"You're talking in clichés again," grumbled Gino, backing up and gesturing with his gun.

"Well, you won't," she said angrily. "Cliché or not, you'll not prosper!"

Gino looked faintly amused and called out to Lefty to get up and rewire the prisoners again. "This time, do it right," he added.

"I did do it right, boss," Lefty complained. But he climbed up to the balcony, picked up the roll of wire, and dutifully rewired Zac and Julie to the railing, this time. Only with twice as much wire and a lot of twistings.

"What's this?" Lefty said to no one, bending over to pick up the leatherbound book on the floor. Gino didn't notice. He was going back down the steps, stuffing his huge automatic back into its holster.

"Uh, that's mine," Zac said to Lefty.

"Wait a minute," Lefty said without heat, thumbing the book open. "I used to read a lot. There's not much else to do in jail, except pump iron and play checkers." He looked up at Zac and said, "I read all the comics I could get my hands on, and there's a pile of them!"

"Good, uh, good for you. You can just stuff it back in my pocket here," Zac said, turning his hip toward Lefty. But the crook didn't notice.

"What is this thing, anyway? Ain't no paperback. What's this stuff?" His lips moved silently for a moment, then he brightened. "Okay, I get it, it's a kind of recipe book, sorta."

"Sorta. You wouldn't be interested."

"Zac, what is going on?" Julie whispered.

"Nothing."

"Men!" She gave him a dark, angry look.

Exhausted, Merlin closed the door to think. He had a feeling there was trouble ahead.

Lefty started reading titles as he leafed idly through the book. "Hey, *Bathsheba's Beauty Secrets . . . Wart and Wen Removal the Byzantine Way . . . How to Design a Shield Boss to Repel Creatures Not of Living Flesh* . . . What's that mean? Hey, kid, this ain't no cookbook, this is a weird book."

He wandered away a few steps and continued to read, his voice only a muttered whisper. Zac could only catch a few words. ". . . Bellona, wife of Mars . . . cantharides . . . Boniface the Fat . . . Aurora . . . chain mail . . . the bones of sparrows killed by lightning . . . summer solstice . . . eastward-facing gargoyles . . . Hippalectryon . . . *putrefactio* . . . keepers of the threshold . . . boy, this is strange stuff . . ."

"Boring stuff," Zac said, keeping his voice low. "Just slip it in here and—"

"Zac, what's going on? No one tells me anything!"

"Julie, be quiet!" Zac whispered.

"Be quiet? That's always what they say. Be quiet. Sit still. Later, dear. This isn't for girls, dear. You wouldn't be interested. You're just a girl and girls don't do this kind of thing." She thrust her face close to Zac's. "Bull-feathers, Zac Rogers!"

Zac looked at Gino, who glanced frowningly up at them, as he tried to quiet Julie down. "I'll explain later, Julie."

"I'll explain later, Julie," Julie said mockingly.

"Lead is a metal associated with Saturn," Lefty read. "Alchemists employed the image of a dove to . . . what's an alchemist? he asked Zac.

"Uh, it's, it's like a druggist. You know, in England they call them chemists?"

"Oh." Lefty turned a page and his face brightened. "Hey, neat. *How to Change Lead into More Precious Material.*"

"Uh, that's not what you think," Zac said quickly.

"Sure it is. I saw them movies and stuff. Lead into gold." He started reading and as Zac tried to interrupt, Lefty waved the gun in his face, but didn't bother to even look. He stumbled over some of the words and had to start again. "I'll have gold bullets just like the Long Stranger."

"Silver," Zac said automatically. "The Lone Ranger had silver bullets."

"Whatever. Shut up, kid, and let me do this

right." Gun in hand, Lefty started reading, his lips moving slowly.

Zac groaned and rolled his eyes. Where was a magician when you needed one?

The needed magician was leaning against the steel door only a few feet away, his head throbbing like Sugar Ray's punching bag. "If only I could give Zac my powers," he muttered, his voice thick. "Even a fraction of my powers, just for a moment. I trust him to use them well." What was that spell Ulric had give him? So long ago, so far away ... he'd never had use for it before ... it was just a temporary thing, anyway, like eating a candy bar for quick energy. Something to give his apprentice the little extra— "Aha!"

As Merlin remembered the ancient spell, he flashed it through his mind. A temporary thing ... all that is needed, he thought. Force away the pain, send the thoughts through the steel and concrete ...

Lefty read the ritual through, then stopped.

Nothing happened. He tucked the book under one arm and broke open the cylinder on his .38 revolver. Then he extracted a cartridge and looked at the bullet.

"Hey!" he said with delight. "Lookit,

silver!" He held the bullet close to Zac in triumph. "Look, silver. Not gold maybe, but what the hey."

"Aluminum," Zac said. He tried to conceal his surprise at Lefty working any kind of spell at all. Maybe the crook was an adept and didn't know it. It wouldn't surprise him, Zac thought—everything else was going whacky tonight.

"Aluminum what?" Lefty said suspiciously.

"Aluminum bullets. Not silver, aluminum."

"Lefty looked at the slug. "How ya know?"

"Does it weigh less or more than the old bullet?"

Lefty fished in his coat pocket and found another cartridge. He tested their weight, then frowned at the silver-tipped cartridge. "Aluminum." He pulled out all the other slugs in the gun. All now had aluminum tips. He frowned at Zac. "This is some kinda trick, ain't it? You switched slugs."

"No, I . . . Then Zac thought about what he was saying. He *did* want to case suspicion on the authenticity of the magic primer. "What did you expect? You thought that was some kind of magic formula or something?" He put a lot of derision in his voice. "Boy, are you dumb!"

"Oh, yeah, well, I think you pulled some kinda switch. I'm gonna try this book again."

Zac groaned. He turned to Julie and whispered, "We've got to do something!"

"Oh?" she responded archly. "We've got to do something? Why 'we,' Zachary? I thought you were doing just fine without little me."

"Julie, we're in trouble here—"

"And you want my help, is that it?"

"Well, sure, we're in trouble, or hadn't you noticed?"

"So later on, when you rescue us, you'll be the hero and I'll be the—"

"What's all this?" Gino was growling at them from the floor below, his face like an irritated bulldog.

"Nothing, nothing," Zac said quickly.

"See that it stays nothing, punk." Gino went back to his pacing.

"Did he just say something in Latin?" Julie asked in a hushed voice, looking at Lefty.

"No. Yes. I wasn't listening. Maybe. Uh, Mister Lefty, that book is kind of personal, y'know, like a diary and, um, well, I really don't like people looking through it."

"You keep a diary?" Julie said in some surprise, but the following smile had a lot of interest in it. "Can I see it?"

"Mister Lefty, please . . . huh?"

"Buzz off, kid. Oh, this one sounds good. *"The Deliverance of Desired Objects*. Oh, yeah. That I like," he said with a wide grin.

Julie was smiling, too. "Harry Barker," she sighed.

"Who?" Zac asked automatically, twitching instead of fluttering his fingers, which were attached to his pinioned hands.

"Harry Barker, silly, of Raw Material. Now there's a desired . . ."

"Julie!" Zac said, slightly shocked.

"What's the matter, Zac, can't a girl have someone she digs, too? All the boys have. Fair's fair."

"Yeah, but." He stopped. Fair was fair. But not now! Zac turned around to try and talk Lefty out of reading anything from the book and found it was too late.

". . . the spiral path!" Lefty finished with a flourish.

Poof!

Poof!

Two poofs, Zac thought, looking around.

"Hey, what's the meaning of this?" A tall blonde in a slinky, red-sequinned evening dress stood at the entrance to one of the side rooms. She had on red-sequined shoes and long, dangly red earrings.

Lefty was staring at the woman with his mouth open, and so was Zac, but at least Zac suspected why she had suddenly appeared. Julie looked, sniffed and turned abruptly away. Then her eyes popped open and she screamed.

"Harry Barker!"

"Hello, luv," said the tall, emaciated young man with the long, dark hair. He was wearing a leather jacket with at least twelve visible zippers, skintight purple trousers, and high cowboy boots of snakeskin and silver. He looked up and down the chamber. "We've been touring for a solid month. I thought I was on my way home—I want to sleep. Why were we booked in here?"

"Harry Barker!" Julie screamed again.

"What's going on?" Gino roared as he charged up the steps, gun in hand. He stopped abruptly, his eyes snapping from the attractive blonde to the sleepy, skinny English musician. "Lefty, who the blue blazes are these people? How'd they get in here?"

"Uh . . . uh . . . uh . . ."

"Lefty!"

"Boss, I dunno. I was reading, I look up, here they are."

"What are they doing here? This place got some kind of secret passages in it or some-

thing? Bozo! Charlie! Get up here!" He
pointed at the side rooms. "Search in there.
Tap the walls. Find out how they got in here!'

Gino strode across to the musician, who
was beginning to droop. "You! Listen up!
How did you get in here? Who are you?"

"He's Harry Barker!" screamed Julie.

"Who's Harry Barker?" Gino asked, looking at the fast-wilting skinny man.

"Oh, deliver me from men!" Julie said.
"Harry Barker of Raw Material!" she said
loudly.

Gino looked him over. "Some raw material.
This dude's out on his feet. What's he on?" He
poked the gun muzzle in Harry's chest.
"Hey! You! What are you doing here?"

Harry slipped slowly, but elegantly to the
floor, where he stretched out and crossed his
hands on his chest, smiling. "I must be
dreaming."

Gino looked at him in disgust. Then he
whirled and strode across the balcony to the
petulant blonde in red. "Okay, sister, what's
up?"

"Who're you, buster?" the woman demanded. Without waiting for an answer, she
sneered at everyone present. "Boy, this is
the lousiest backstage I was ever in! Where's

the john? Where's my dressing room? I step out for one second—one second, mind you—and I get lost! Where's my manager?" Still without waiting for an answer, she yelled loud enough to make Gino take a step backward. "*Murray!*" I'll get you for this, Murray! Booking me into the O'Farrell was bad enough, but into *this* sewer!"

She looked around, steaming, and Gino turned to Lefty. "Who's this ding-a-ling?"

"That's Suzzan," Lefty gulped.

"Who's Suzanne? Suzanne what?"

"Suzzan, boss. *The* Suzzan."

"Oh, are you one of my fans?" Suzzan's voice was all honey. "Get me a drink, will you? Stop looking—look at my face. A drink." She snapped her fingers. "Make it snappy. You—yeah, you—put that gun away. They make me nervous."

"Harry Barker," Julie sighed, looking at the recumbent musician. "Right here. If I weren't tied up . . ."

"Listen, bimbo," began Gino.

"Hey!" snapped Suzzan loudly. To Lefty she made a complaint. "Who is this jerk? He run this crummy joint?" Again, without waiting, she snapped back at Gino. "Listen, fatso, I'm a headliner, see? People come from all over to see me, wherever I play."

"Uh-huh, uh-huh," Lefty said.

"I get top dollar and I'm worth it. You got any complaints, you talk to my agent. But first you better talk to my public. Where's the stage?" she demanded of Lefty.

"Stage?"

"Where's the stage? Where do I work?"

"We, uh, we don't have any stage here," Lefty said nervously.

"Murray!" Suzzan bellowed angrily. "Murray! I'll get you for this! You booked me into a sewer, Murray! It's just like the Tropicana Bar all over again, Murray! No stage, no dressing room! "No, thanks, buster! I know those deals."

"Uh, Miss Suzzan, I wonder if I could, uh—"

"Buzz off, buster. No autographs, no pictures. Not in this place! Murray!" She turned and walked into the cable room. Almost at once she walked out, fuming. "What kind of dressing room is that supposed to be? It's got wires going through it and lumps of clay and some nincompoop tapping on concrete walls!"

Without waiting she strode down the steps and over to the door. When she found it was locked, she snapped at Lefty. "You! Open this up! That trick won't work with me!"

Lefty scurried down the steps, leaving an astounded Gino staring after him. "Miss Suzzan, you can't just go out there."

"Sonny, I make my living going out there. My public is waiting. Now open up! *Arriba, arriba!*"

Lefty fumbled with the lock and pulled the door open. Without looking she smiled a wide, red, and very phony, smile at Lefty who all but melted. "Thank you. You can be secretary of my fan club." And out the door she went.

"Close the door!" Gino yelled.

The soft *pong* of the metal door closing echoed through the room.

"Harry Barker," sighed Julie.

Chapter Ten

Merlin watched the woman come out into the night. She looked surprised, then angry. She marched off, elbows swinging, muttering something about a dread villain named Murray.

Merlin sighed. Things were not going well at all. It was something like a dream, he thought, where events are out of control and you cannot change them very much.

This was a very uncomfortable feeling for Merlin. He'd been in situations before where he actually worried about surviving but he hadn't been so confused. He had known what Morgen le Fey was up to, and Vivien and Nyneve, even Modred, the illegitimate spawn of the union between Arthur and

Morgen le Fey. Or the time the dead dragon turned out to be very much alive. Or when Xerxes proved stronger and more dangerous then he had thought. But he had not been so muddled, and his thinking had never been so erratic.

"Pull yourself together, old man," Merlin grumbled aloud. "Time is running out."

Merlin rose from his hiding place and went unsteadily across the pavement to the steel door. He leaned against it, palms flat, and there was a ripple down the length of his body, a sweep of darkness, swift and discordant.

Merlin grunted.

The frogs began coming up out of the drain.

Ribbit. Ribbit. *Ribbit.*

"Boss!" Bozo yelped. "Boss, lookit!"

"Stomp 'em!" Gino growled.

"Urg!" Bozo said. The very idea sickened him.

More frogs came up, hopping out to look around, then hopping on again. Twelve, fifteen, twenty. "Put something over that drain!" Gino yelled. Twenty-four, thirty, thirty-six.

"I ain't got nothing," Bozo said, retreating

before the green horde. Forty, fifty, fifty-five.

"Don't let them get to Harry!" Julie said.

"Sit on it!" Gino ordered.

"What?" Bozo said from against the wall. "*You* sit on it!" He retreated up the steps.

Ribbit. Ribbit. RIBBIT!

Sixty-five, seventy-five, ninety. The blips of green and yellow kept spitting up from the drain. One hundred, one-ten, one-twenty.

"Do something!" Gino yelled at his men, who were retreating up the steps. None of them offered to do anything.

Croak. Hop. *Croak*. Hop. *Croak*. Hop.

Zac looked around. Merlin's work, for certain. Yet it *could* be a natural occurrence. A later investigation might show a plague of frogs in the south bay, forced up a drainage pipe . . .

Ribbit. *Ribbitribbitribbitribbit*.

"It's like one o' them movies," Lefty said, a quaver in his voice. "*The Revenge of the Frog People* or sumpin'."

Gino gave him a dark look. "Okay, then, hero, you go down and stop up that drain. Use your jacket."

"Uh . . ."

Silently, Gino pulled out his automatic and pointed the weapon at his second in command. Lefty started down the steps, gingerly kicking frogs out of his path. They hopped aside, their eyes swiveling to follow him.

RIBBIT. RIBBIT. RIBBIT.

Lefty peeled off his jacket. "There must be two hunnert of these things," he complained. He brushed the frogs aside, wadding up his jacket. One came flying out of the drain, banked off his face, and sailed off to be the first one onto the balcony.

"Ugh!" Julie exclaimed.

Ribbit.

Lefty jammed the jacket down into the drain, then stomped unmercifully as hundreds of froggy eyes watched him. Then he ran for the stairs, making little squeaking noises. The frogs hopped leisurely out of his path.

Splat!

Lefty's jacket exploded from the drain, followed by two dozen frogs in tight formation.

Ribbit. Ribbit. Ribbit.

Gino pointed down. Lefty shook his head. Gino pointed the gun. Lefty gulped, but shook his head in terrified negation of the order. He held onto the balcony railing with both hands.

Gino gave up. "Let the cops worry about them," he grumbled. "They'll be here soon.

We're all set. Door locked. Handy pair of hostages. A plan all figured out. A boat stashed. A hideout in exotic Sacramento. A fence to clean the money." He looked around. "Never mind them froggies. Just listen for the cops."

For a long moment they all just stared down at the frogs. "Hey, girlie," Gino leered, "maybe you kiss one o' them frogs, you get yourself a prince, huh? A whole roomful of princes!" He was the only one that laughed.

Ribbit. Ribbit. Ribbit.

Two hundred fifty, three hundred, three-fifty.

They were on the steps, a few on the balcony. Some sat and watched, some hopped. There were frogs sitting on frogs.

"Don't let them get near Harry," Julie pleaded to Gino.

The thug didn't respond for awhile, then one frog hopped all the way from the floor and landed on Gino's shoe. He kicked the little amphibian off and growled at Charlie and Bozo. "Get the Limey on his feet."

The two crooks, both battered, soaking wet, and terminally disheveled from all their head-bangings, fumblings, rain encounters, and natural-born slovenly natures, stumbled over and lifted the limp musician up.

"Whuzzat?" Harry said. "Time? Who's opening act? Not the Freckled Bee-Joes again?" He looked from Charlie to Bozo for confirmation.

Neither thug answered, then, propping him up against the cement wall, stood with a hand on each shoulder, keeping him up and watching the frogs come over the balcony edge, one by one.

Ribbit.

Harry Barker stared at the green creatures for a minute, then closed his eyes. "Go away," Harry said wearily. "You don't exist, I don't see you, go back to where the snakes come from."

"Harry . . ." Julie said softly.

"Eh? Oh, hello, luv. Only one of you? Where are the others, luv?" He looked around. "Where's the band, hey?" He raised his voice. "Bob? Shaw? Jimmy? Sleech? Where are ya, lads? Time to go make music!"

Julie tried to explain, but by her third word Harry Barker had dropped his head to his chest and started snoring.

He went limp and it was all Charlie and Bozo could do to keep him from banging his head. They let Harry sink down and stretched him out, sighing. "Some hostage he'll be," muttered Charlie irritably.

"Harry ..." Julie said sadly, staring at him.

After a moment she turned to look at Zac. "And what are you doing to—" She stopped, staring. Zac Rogers had been strangely silent through all of this, his silence unnoticed in the confusion.

Zac stood stiffly, eyes closed. At first Julie thought he was scared stiff at the invasion of frogs, but she quickly saw he was unaware of them. There was one sitting at each foot, in fact.

"Zac? Zac!" She saw his lips moving, as if he was trying to talk, or the way some people read to themselves. "Zac?"

The frogs began to hop faster. They came up the steps in a flowing river, hopping and riding on each other's backs. Ribbiting loudly, they flooded over the balcony edge, flowing like a green, lumpy river past and through the six humans. Gino yelled and fired several rounds into the advancing horde.

Charlie tried to climb higher. Bozo gulped and backed up, tripping and falling into the rippling river of amphibians. He screamed once, then a two-pound frog settled in his mouth. Lefty tried to climb up on the railing, slipped, and thumped down the other side.

Losing his grip, he fell screaming into the squirming frog pit.

And not one frog touched Julie or Zac.

The green river flowed along the balcony and down the southern steps, across the floor, over the wriggling form of Lefty, and up the other steps, across the balcony, and down the left-hand steps.

Again and again and again.

Ribbit. Ribbit. Ribbit.

A stampede of frogs.

A carpet of speckled green.

Encrusting the balcony.

Bozo fought his way to his hands and knees, spitting out the frog. He slipped on the frogs that were under him. He bumped and shook as he was borne along to the stairs, where he went face down in a screaming slide, to tumble into the seething frog pit and be covered with the jade-colored hoppers.

Charlie had his feet swept out from under him. He fell heavily, just missing squashing a clutch of frogs and Harry Barker. He scrambled to his feet, kicking frogs away, but soon fell again as nineteen two-pound frogs hopped up on his chest and face. He, too, was taken, yelling and trying to cling to Zac's legs and the railing.

Unceremoniously, he was sent down the chute of frogbacks to the pit. And still the frogs hopped up and across and down, up and across and down.

Ba-lam! Ka-pow!

"Get away from me!" Gino screamed. He aimed his automatic into the carpet of tailless amphibians and pulled the trigger.

Click.

Gino bellowed, reversed the gun and started striking down at the bug-eyed creatures. He smashed his gun into the cement as the target frog hopped aside. The gun was wrenched from Gino's grasp and went reeling off, to be buried under a frog pack.

Cursing, Gino stood erect. His eyes were wild as he looked around. Frogs were bumping against his legs as he clung to the balcony rail. "Lefty! Get up, Lefty! Bozo! Charlie!"

There was no answer, only a heaving of the frog mantle covering the bottom level.

Ribbit. Ribbit. Ribbit.

Gino looked at Julie and Zac. "This is your fault! I had a nice little caper going here until you two got into the act!" His hand went into his pocket and it came out grasping a switchblade.

He flipped the knife open with a practiced

gesture. Light reflected off the gleaming blade. A dozen frogs hopped up onto Gino's back. He staggered, but shrugged them off. His eyes were wild.

"You! You're jinxes! But I'm going to fix that!"

Gino started to lunge forward, but three dozen frogs leaped onto his back. He jerked and slammed against the railing, almost but not quite losing his grip on the deadly knife. He flung them off him with violent motions of his shoulders and took another step toward the trussed-up couple.

A fat frog, weighing at least three pounds, leaped high into the air and kicked out at Gino's face. But the street-wise thug, veteran of a hundred back-alley fights, ducked. The frog fell to the rippled sea of frogs below, his brave attempt a failure.

Gino growled. It was an animal growl, a cry of fear and anger. He kicked aside a dozen frogs that were sitting on each other's backs before him. Two dozen hopped in to make a bigger pile. A small frog started crawling up Gino's right trouser leg. With a roar Gino lifted his legs and shook out the frog—as another frog squeezed up his left trouser leg.

Bellowing, Gino started wading through

the barrier of croaking, kicking, slipping, hopping frogs. His knife made vicious swipes before him, just missing the ever-higher-climbing frogs.

The frogs at the bottom of the almost waist-high mound were hunkered down, groaning under the weight of their fellows. The ones at the top kept leaping toward Gino's face.

"Arrrrr—!" the burly thug yelled, slicing back and forth with the knife. But the blade made no contact whatsoever. Before him the frogs piled higher; behind Gino they leaped upon his back, his head, landing on his shoulders, pummeling him with their webbed feet, whacking him in leaps past his black-clothed body.

Julie screamed. Zac quivered, staring.

Ribbit. Ribbit . . .

Gino waded inexorably closer, his red eyes wild, his knife swinging closer and closer to the tender young flesh of Julie Potter.

Merlin was exhausted. His head hurt. The power drain of forcing the spell through the thick steel was taking its toll.

I'm not the wizard I once was, he told himself. Not with a head like a dropped watermelon.

He felt himself weakening. His head pulsed with agonizing regularity.

His fingers felt hot; his feet felt cold.

Things got blurry.

Things stayed blurry.

Until they went black.

Chapter Eleven

Gino kicked aside the pyramid of frogs before him. They leaped away, croaking, and no new attack force surged up. His eyes staring, Gino pressed closer, his knife pulling back for a final, vicious slice . . . and stopped.

The frogs were moving. Back. Going down the drain in a steady, rippling stream. Already the balcony was almost clear. He could see Lefty's back and Bozo's knee. "What the—"

Gino stared as the frogs flowed in a steady line down and out. Gone. Charlie was uncovered, Lefty was moving, Bozo was rubbing his face.

And then there was one.

One frog. Not a very big one, but the last one left.

There were no more green amphibians, just one speckled creature. *Ribbit*, it croaked, and jumped. Down the drain and gone.

The big room was quiet.

"Boss," Lefty said, sitting up. "This is the screwiest job we've ever been on. Not even when we found we were in the police chief's house has it been so weird."

"Weird," agreed Bozo, sitting up.

"Weird," Charlie said, shaking his head.

Gino seemed to have forgotten the knife in his hand. He looked around, blinking. "What happened?"

Harry Barker groaned and sat up on one elbow.

"Harry," Julie sighed.

"Gig over?" Harry asked. "What do they serve here, anyway, hey?"

"Shuddup," Gino said without much heat. He sagged against the railing and seemed to see the switchblade for the first time. Carefully, he folded the weapon and returned it to his pocket. "Bozo, bring me my gun, will ya?"

"Sure, boss." Bozo scooped up the weapon, wiped the metal on his still-wet clothing and came up the steps to hand it over. Gino pulled the clip and dropped it into a pocket. He pulled out a second clip and rammed it home.

"I never done so much shooting on a job in my life," he muttered. He looked suspiciously at the weapon, then wrenched off the useless silencer.

"Where are the cops?" Lefty asked. He looked at his watch.

"They oughta be here by now."

Merlin heard it first. Distant sirens. "Oh, no," he said, sitting up in the doorway. Everything seemed to whirl. I must have passed out, he told himself.

RRRrrrrrrRRRrrrrrrRRR . . .

But closer still was the burring blurt of a moped.

Leo Samuels came zipping around the nearest corner and chugged up the street. Merlin clawed at the edges of the recessed door and got to his feet, his head pounding like the hammer of Thor.

Things were hanging around Leo's neck. Long strings of sausages. Some of the sausages were only halves. These were at the ends of the shortest strings.

Then Merlin heard the barking dogs.

"Quick!" Leo said, tumbling off the moped. He lifted the bobbing links from his neck and gathered them into his arms. "I lost some but there should be enough to—"

His head snapped around as a howling pack of dogs scampered around the corner after him. "Urp!" he exclaimed and thrust the meaty mess into Merlin's hands.

"What are these for?" the old magician said, frowning. "Are we having a picnic?"

Leo stared at him goggle-eyed. "You told me to get sausages! Fifty feet of sausages!" He looked down the street at the dog pack. Dobermans, too. He hated Dobermans. Poodles, a Great Dane, collies, two golden retrievers, a Dalmatian, several terriers, and bringing up the rear, a beagle and a bulldog.

"Mister Merlin," Leo said in a quavering voice, I'll . . . I'll distract them, lead them off. You do what you have to do."

Leo jumped back on his moped and tried to crank it up. The baying of the hounds and the approaching police hastened his second try. "I had to run a few red lights," Leo explained. Then the motor caught and he went buzzing off.

As he did, Merlin threw aside the sausages.

Which fell across the back of the moped, well-tangled in the basket, the license plate, and the tail light.

The dogs, barking, yapping, baying, and yipping, galloped by in pursuit. A few moments later, so did two police cars. They never even noticed the old bum leaning against the wall.

"What was all that?" Merlin said to no one. He touched his throbbing head.

The sounds of the dogs had not penetrated the cable anchorage, but the shriek of the sirens had. All of Gino's men had guns in their hands. Gino waved his automatic and said, "Steady. Keep to the plan. They'll try to talk us out first. They'll stall for time. But—"

"Boss," Lefty said. He pointed to the outside. "The cops went on by."

"Why?" Gino said in astonishment. "If that's a trick, it's a dumb one. What are they up to?"

"Give yourself up," Julie said. "Throw yourself on the mercy of the court!"

That made Gino, Lefty, and Charlie laugh. Bozo was rubbing his head. "Forget it, sister," Gino said. "We're in it all the way. But you can't trust a cop," he said to his men. "They'll tell you anything, promise you anything, then zap you. Cops are just not honest." His men nodded in sad agreement.

Julie looked at Zac, who was being very quiet again, eyes closed. Gino walked over to the stairs. "Listen at the door, Bozo," he said.

Julie looked at Harry Barker. "Mister Barker? Uh, Harry?"

"Yeah, luv? Want an old autograph, do you? On what part?"

"Harry, do something," Julie insisted.

"Oh?" He looked around. "Where's m'axe, luv? Me guitar?" He looked behind him, staggered, and swayed. "My new hit, hey? *Bigfoot's Romances*, hey? Or something from m'album, *Frankenstein of Sunnybrook Farm*? Where's Jimmy? Where's the Geek?"

He staggered some more, bumping into Gino. Who was pushed forward. Who took a step down to regain his balance. Whose foot hit the chunk blasted from the cement step when he had fired at Zac earlier.

With a hoarse cry Gino fell down the steps. Charlie tried to grab him, got a whack across the bump on his head, and fell back unconscious.

Bozo turned to help his gangland leader and ran smack into Lefty, who was attempting to do the same thing. Gino fell across Charlie and his gun went off.

Ka-Pow!

Lefty and Bozo both lurched out of the way—smashing into each other again, cracking heads. With a double groan, they fell unconscious to the floor.

Gino tried to stand, tripped over Charlie's outflung hand, and went face-first into the wall.

From the balcony, Harry Barker surveyed the damage. "Oh, I say, I'm terribly sorry. . . ."

Zac smiled.

Julie bleated desperately, "Harry, get us out of these wires!"

"Wires?"

"These wires!" Julie said, jerking on her bonds.

"Oh." He swayed toward them. "Say, you look a little young to be keeping this kind of company. Nice-looking bird, though. Who's your favorite group?"

"Raw Material. Harry, the wire?"

"Righto, luv. Say, you, too?" he said to Zac, who had a happy and serene look.

"Hmmm?" Zac said as the wires were untwisted. He looked down at the unconscious quartet and could not suppress a faint giggle.

"My hero!" Julie said. Zac started to turn around, forming a modest expression, ready to receive his just due. And found Julie with her arms around Harry Barker. "You saved us," she said. "You took care of all of them!"

"Oh? Well, uh, nothing to it, really." He peered down at the unmoving four. "Bad ones, hey? Serves you right!" he shouted down at them.

Zac turned away. There was a turmoil in his chest. To tell or not to tell.

It hurt, but he made up his mind. He walked slowly down the stairs, stepped over Gino, and went over to the big steel door. He unlocked it and swung it out, then stopped and looked up at Julie, who was kissing Harry Barker all over his face.

"Easy, luv, easy, there's plenty to go around. You just let me get some rest and then we'll talk about—"

Then his eyes rolled up and he fell slowly and elegantly to the floor. Julie screeched. Zac blinked. It hadn't been his doing. He looked out in the street.

Merlin was standing in a thunderstorm, soaking wet.

The thunderstorm was covering an area about as big as a bed. When he moved to get out from under, the dark cloud moved with him. A tiny lightning bolt, about as long as a finger, crackled above his head.

"I'm doing something wrong," Merlin said, his hand to his head.

Wearily, Zac trudged out and across the street. He reached in through the rain and took Merlin's hand. "Come on, Max." The rain stopped and the cloud dissipated. "Let's go call the cops and get your head fixed."

They left a wet trail down the street.

In the distance they could hear the yelping of dogs.

"Turned out the deejay thought the record was a hoax," Zac said, sitting in Max's living room.

The old man smiled and touched the bandage on his head lightly. "This wasn't. It was a lot of trouble fixing all those places where my magic went awry, but there was one thing I couldn't fix."

Max's gaze went to the newspaper lying the coffee table. In bold black letters, it said, ROCK STAR FOILS BOMBERS.

Zac sighed. "I know, I know," he said, holding up his hand. "What have I learned from this?" He made a face and nodded ruefully, glancing at Merlin. "Oh, stop smiling! I learned that magic must be carefully done and not promiscuously. That it is necessary to keep our identity secret. That guns scare me. That the best thing to do is make magic look like a natural, if coincidental, occurrence."

He gestured toward the newspapers. "Barker's PR man has the whole story, how Barker suspected the bad guys and sneaked in to rescue Miss Julie Potter and an unidentified companion. And how, by successfully faking inebriation, he threw them off the track until he pounced. He crossed the cable anchorage like a giant jungle cat and vanquished the villains in a short but brutal session of desperate combat, four to one, with the other guys fully armed and desperate. They fought like cornered rats but were no match for Harry Barker's graceful karate movements. Four men are in custody with an APB out for a fourth suspect. An arrest is expected at any moment."

Zac ended his approximate quotation from the news report and made another wry grimace. There was a long, deep silence.

"You did all right," Merlin said at last. "Not bad for a beginner, actually."

"Maybe. But there was other apprentice material in there with me. Did you know that Lefty is an adept? I couldn't believe it!"

Merlin chuckled. "No. Unfortunately, it's more like I'm inept! I meant that energy spell to land on you. But somehow in my weakened state, and because the spell had to travel through so much concrete and steel, it went off in Lefty's direction. And anyway, you did a good job of covering up."

Zac laughed, obviously relieved. "I was pinch-hitting for the best." "No mention of you," he added, pointing again to the newspaper. "Gino and those guys think it was the most incredible string of bad luck they had ever heard of."

Merlin smiled and waited. There was something else on Zac's mind, he could tell.

"There's one thing I don't understand," Zac said.

"And that is?"

"Well . . . since, you know, I became your apprentice . . . well, I—"

"You looked me up." Merlin smiled. The boy nodded. "And you have questions?"

"Uh-huh. Look, I don't doubt that you're Merlin and all, but, well . . . uh . . . there was Nyneve . . . ."

"Ah," Merlin said, a sad expression crossing his face, one of bittersweet memory. "So, that story has been concerning you all along?"

Zac nodded. "She, uh ... well, this Sir Pellinore brought her to Arthur's court and you, uh ..."

"I fell for her hook, line, and sinker." Merlin sighed, smiling ruefully. "She was one of the damsels of the Lady in the Lake, you know."

"You told King Arthur all that was going to happen? At least, that's what the legends say."

Merlin nodded.

"Then *why* did you let her?"

"I warned Arthur, yes, for all the good it did him."

"You went with her, you taught her all the magical arts."

Merlin nodded, his eyes looking into the distant past.

"You taught her spells which could not be broken by any means, you have her antidotes against magic, and ..." Zac hesitated. "And you made a wonderful room under a rock cliff ..."

"For us to be alone together." Merlin sighed, remembering.

"And when you stepped into it, she stepped back," Zac said. "And she cast an awful spell that cannot be broken by any means. The passage was closed and you were ... trapped inside ... uh ..."

"For all time to come?" Merlin said with a slight smile. He sighed. "That's the legend, all right. Of course, there's another—Vivien, who is supposed to have put me into either a thorn bush or a tower, to come out only when England had need of me again."

The old magician shook his head. "When you've been around awhile, they hang a lot of things on you you didn't do and they ignore some of the things you did do."

"But . . . uh . . . well, did Nyneve . . .?"

"Oh, yes," Merlin said, shrugging. "It was really a great disappointment. You should learn something from that, Zachary. She was just after my power. She was just . . . how do you say it these days? She was just putting me off."

"On. Putting you on."

"That's what she did, all right."

"You were, uh, sealed up and all?"

"Uh-huh." Merlin seemed saddened by his thoughts.

"Then how did you—"

"Get out?" An impish grin brightened his face. "Well, you see, I taught her everything she knew . . . but . . ." His grin widened. "I didn't teach her everything *I* knew!"